THE MAN IN THE HOTEL CEILING

C.G. LAMBERT

First paperback edition August 2021

Published by Clamp Ltd

Set in Junicode and Trade Gothic

Cover Art by Nick Castle

ISBN 978-1-914531-10-1 Paperback

ISBN 978-1-914531-11-8 Hardback

ISBN 978-1-914531-12-5 ePUB

www.cglambert.com

www.clamp.pub

For Mum & Dad

For Mum & Dad

CONTENTS

ACKNOWLEDGMENTS

Even self-published novels have many people helping—and while every mistake is my own, the following people have been most helpful with their contributions:

Thanks to my beta readers—Andrew Grenfell, Todd Gault & Parth Munjani for their insights and feedback.

Special thanks to my Sensitivity reader, Nicola Soremekun and my Military Advisors Jason Watkins and my friend from the Princess of Wales's Royal Regiment. Expert advice is worth its weight in gold.

Thanks again to my Editor, Michael Thorn for his gentle guidance and advice.

Thanks again to Nick Castle for the great cover. And his patience!

And always, thanks to my First Reader.

THE PUB

Mike walked into the pub. It was almost empty, due in equal parts to it being a Monday night and the result of midwinter rain driving the CBD office workers home rather than dallying in the city. As a result, Auckland had emptied out, leaving the wind tunnel streets to the homeless, the students and those few working late. Mike was an inch shorter than average but he'd made a point of eating well and kept fit with frequent visits to the gym. Whenever he found himself admiring his physique in the mirror, he would remember his tailor measuring him for suits. Nothing brought him back down to earth more swiftly than the Trinidadian tailor calling out his shortcomings for his assistant to write down. Left shoulder dropped by an inch, right leg an inch longer than the left—that sort of thing.

A large Maori behind the bar absentmindedly wiped the counter with a cloth, lost in thought. He started when he noticed that Mike had come in, but smiled welcomingly. One other customer sat on a stool at the bar, turning to inspect the new arrival. He looked like a pumpkin that had been left out too long after Halloween—a bald head, except for a pair of shocking white tufts at the ears, and a sunken mouth devoid of most of its teeth.

"Can I have a pint of lager, please?" Mike asked, as he sat at a stool at the bar.

"Coming right up," answered the barman. "English?" he asked.

Mike smiled and nodded. His accent wasn't quite what you would hear on the BBC, but it was close.

"'Ere! Where's your mates?" squawked the pumpkin, squinting at Mike.

Surprised to be so greeted, Mike shrugged. "I don't know what you mean."

"The Scotsman and the Irishman? You're English aren't you?"

The barman looked up from pouring Mike's drink. "Steve, stop bothering him." He half apologised while explaining. "'An Englishman, an Irishman and a Scotsman walked into a bar...' It's the beginning of many jokes, right?"

"Although are you really English? You don't look English."

Mike looked over sharply. "And what exactly do you mean by that... friend?" His tone was anything but friendly.

"Where are you from originally?"

Mike blinked in surprise. He hadn't been in the country for 48 hours and he was already dealing with questions that would start fights back in London. He looked over at the barman who was just finishing pouring. Mike made eye contact and raised an eyebrow and the barman seemed to remember his responsibilities. "That's $9 mate. Steve, you're going to have to leave. You can't go around asking questions like that."

"Was it something I said? I was just asking a question. You can't say anything these days."

"Finish your drink and then go."

Steve swallowed what was left in his glass, though truth be told it was just froth and dregs which he had been nursing for the better part of ten minutes. Something told Mike that Steve was the barfly type who would use a drink-an-hour as an excuse to talk to someone. He placed the glass overly carefully on the bar and grabbed his jacket to go. "Yeah, you lot stick together, don't you?" he called over his shoulder as he left.

The bartender pursed his lips. "Sorry about that, bro. Steve's a dick."

Mike nodded. "Not your fault. Is he that way about the Maori too?" He pronounced Maori in the way typical of the English so that it came out sounding like 'Murray'.

2

The barman started wiping down the bar. "Wouldn't worry me if he did. I'm a Sa," he said with a wink.

"What's a Sa?" asked Mike, unsure of himself and hoping he hadn't caused offence.

"Samoan. It's a Pacific Island, north of New Zealand, near Tonga. Really beautiful."

"Oh, sorry, I just thought—"

"All good bro, it happens all the time. I'm Jim." They shook hands. "Sorry about Steve."

"So, did I just get lucky with Steve? Is he the local racist? Or is that what I've got to look forward to in this lovely country?"

Jim thought for a minute. "Hmmm... are you asking if racism exists in New Zealand? Let me tell you a story. There's a TV game show called Wheel of Fortune—do you know it? Huge in the US and they had a local version with celebrities. You have to guess a phrase and each turn you choose a consonant to see if it's in the phrase. You spin a big wheel for each letter and it comes up with a prize which adds to your points and you can spend the points on vowels. The way you ask for the consonant is you say, 'I would like a B for beer'. Anyways, David Tua was on the show. Samoan boxer. He spins and asks for an 'O for Olsen'—his mate is Olsen Filipina, he's a Samoan Rugby League player. Anyway, the host decides that he had asked for an 'O for awesome' and then everyone picks up on it and mocks him for it. But are they making fun of him for being a stupid boxer or a stupid Islander? Hard to tell, right? What about you?"

"Stop and search. Growing up, the cops always gave me and my mates a hard time. They're only supposed to search if there's probable cause, but there's no oversight. Nobody cares that it's effectively harassment. So anything to do with the cops leaves you with a bad taste in your mouth."

"Yeah, being a bouncer means you get to see the good side of the Police when someone has too much to drink and kicks off, but on my days off..."

Jim trailed off and decided to change topics. "You're a long way from home, though. What brings you to Auckland in the middle of winter?"

"I'm staying in the hotel up there," he said, indicating the hotel above them. "Seeing the sights, seeing what trouble I can get myself into," he smiled. He had a good smile, the white of his teeth contrasting strikingly with what his grandmother had called his Jamaican tan.

Most nights it was just Jim and Mike in the pub. Thursday night was Latin dancing night and the one time Mike had poked his head in, the tension between creepy older men wanting to score and the younger women wanting to learn to dance drove him back to the comfort of his hotel room. Friday night tended to be full of office workers unwinding after a stressful week, while Saturday was the generic weekend crowd. So from Thursday through to the weekend, Jim would switch to working security, a full complement of bartenders taking care of the customers inside. Mike thought that Jim wouldn't need Mike distracting him, so Mike concentrated his visits on the early weeknights when there was nothing else going on.

"Tell me about England," Jim asked one night.

Mike considered that for a while. "It's the only home I've known, but I tell you what, sometimes it's not very welcoming."

"I think I know what you mean," Jim nodded. "It's the little things, right? The vibe changing when you walk in the room, a little more care around the ATM when you're there, different body language."

"Microaggressions."

"Hmm...?"

"It's what they call those little things you just described – microaggressions. But I'm talking about macroaggressions. In the rougher neighbourhoods, the skinny white guys with their mates yelling things from cars. "Go back to where you came from", that sort of thing. Yeah, I don't want to go back to Clapham, thanks. Same here?"

"Hmm...I haven't had anyone yell from a car, but the other stuff builds up after a while, you know? You do get a whole lot of really well-meaning Pakeha showing how 'right on' they are by speaking their Maori to you." He pronounced Maori so it sounded more like 'mouldy'. "Like all brown faces are the same, right? I should learn some German or something and try speaking that to them."

"I'm no good with accents, do Samoans have an accent?"

"They might if they first come over, but my family has been over here since the '70s. What about you?"

"My grandfather came over from Jamaica to London to work on the buses in 1970. My father met my mother at a church dance—her family was also from Jamaica—and I came screaming into the world a year after they'd been married. All very proper. Mum... passed away from complications related to my birth and so I was raised by a somewhat chaotic combination of grandparents, uncles, aunts and my father. I didn't even consider whether that was a normal upbringing, until later on at high school. It turned out a lot of my friends had also only had just one parent. They weren't as lucky with the support of a wider family unit. Some of them had a significantly less positive outcome."

"But what about your Jamaican accent? Did you ever have one?"

"My accent had never been too strong—and as I progressed through school it became less and less pronounced, much to my friends' amusement. As my goals diverged from those of my friends, the loss of the accent was seen by them as part of a betrayal of our shared background. It pissed me off a bit, if I'm telling the truth. It wasn't like I did it on purpose. I concentrated on reinventing myself at University, buckling down and throwing myself at my books. Dad had been so very proud when I graduated with a commerce degree and went to work in Audit at one of the big four accounting firms in the City."

"Oh, good for you!"

"After that, I transferred to Forensics and learned as much as I could about the IT side and found that I had a natural leaning in that direction. I was at the same firm for about five years, before there was a shitty situation and I left. They didn't want me to poach any clients, so they made me go on three months gardening leave, meaning I could spend a month in New Zealand, albeit in the middle of winter."

"Man, they pay you not to go to the office? Maybe I should have paid more attention in class. That's awesome!"

Conversations with Jim were the highlight of the first week for Mike—until he met Rachel.

RACHEL

The elevator pinged on arrival at his floor and he made his way down the corridor towards his room. The corridors were lined with room service trays. Perhaps not every door but close to every other—say two trays every five doors. Some guests had laid a cloth napkin over the remains of their dinner, like some sort of funeral shroud. Others left their tray uncovered, showing carcasses, bones and pizza crusts and a few barely-touched full plates of food.

The identical corridors of the hotel disappeared into the distance. They were neutrally coloured, the off-white paint designed to go with everything. The carpet was a repeating pattern—some sort of Celtic knot which folded back on itself in tasteful dark colours. It meandered across the floor as it made its way forward. Mike giggled as he followed the path across the carpet as if it was a maze. It made his trip to his room twice as long as it needed to be, but he didn't mind because he was very drunk.

The corridors were so similar that the hotel had planted different vases along the walls for navigating purposes. Mike's door was opposite an elegant mock Ming vase in deep emerald, accentuated with gold inlay. If you mapped his route from elevator to room, it would pretty much bounce from vase to vase like Pacman collecting pellets.

The doors to the rooms were extra high—nearly eight feet tall—but the ceiling was even higher, maybe another full foot and a half above the top of the door jam. The airy space, elegant vases and tasteful skirting boards gave the impression of luxury only slightly offset by an empty beer or wine bottle the odd guest had left inside one of the vases.

Mike eventually got to his room and tapped his wallet to the keycard reader. It blinked green and he entered. The room was huge. Each wall was ten metres long. The door opened into one corner of the room which held the kitchenette, and opposite that was the bathroom. Across the other side of the room were enormous windows which stretched the entire length of the wall, affording a view of the car park on the other side of the street. Reg had joked that it had "park" views.

Beyond the car park, you could sneak peeks at the marina and the harbour beyond. The Harbour Bridge was just visible if you craned your neck. The bedroom was a six by six metre square tucked into the corner behind the bathroom—a long walk if you needed a pee in the middle of the night. The rest of the apartment with the high ceilings and the tall windows was normally bathed in natural light from outside, and this late the windows gave a great night view of the cityscape. The large lounge area was tastefully decorated with assorted couches and a dining table, the space broken up by four floor-to-ceiling wooden pillars.

The heavy door closed behind him with a whomph, a cushion of air pressure preventing it from slamming. Mike giggled again. This place was twice the size of his house in High Wycombe, a commuter town northwest of London, and about three times the size of the apartment he'd had when he'd rented in the City. He flopped on the closest couch and reflected on the night he'd had. Yes, it had been a good night.

It had been successful. He'd been sitting at the bar by himself when he'd noticed a couple in one of the booths obviously on a first date. He thought it was only him and Jim present, so had started narrating the possible conversation going on between the couple. He'd been on form and had cracked Jim up, giving each one of the twosome a persona and developing a back story, only pausing when one or other of them came to get a round of drinks or to use the bathroom. In fact, Jim's reactions seemed to be at least ten percent more appreciative than Mike's jokes deserved, but he blamed that on his elegant delivery and accent.

He was twenty minutes into it when a voice from a table behind him had interrupted. "You've got her pretty much right, but apparently he's in middle management at an accountancy firm." He'd turned and found that another of the patrons had been listening to his running commentary. As he squirmed with discomfort, he turned to see if Jim had known that she was listening. Jim's guilty laughing told him that his over-effusive reactions had been based on the fact that she'd been listening in as well.

"I got her right? How do you know?" he asked, turning his attention to the interloper. She had shed her puffer jacket, placing it on the seat beside her. She was in office attire, a white blouse under a smart navy blazer and matching skirt. Pleasant looking, rather than attractive. Like the couple chatting, she seemed to be in her late twenties.

She smiled back. "Maya asked me to come along and make sure she didn't get roofied. First date and all that."

"You're a good friend. Hi, I'm Mike. This is Jim."

"Rachel."

"So I said the guy was a lawyer, didn't I? And he's an accountant? I wonder if there are any clues I missed?"

"They're pretty much the same, so no. What about you? What's an Englishman doing drinking midweek, alone?"

He acted mock offended at her dismissal of Jim. "Jim's here too." But he nodded, accepting her point. "I'm on holiday and despite what they say about Kiwis being friendly, Jim here is the only friend I've made. Of course, this pub is as far as I've ventured, so I shouldn't be too hard on the country!"

"How long are you here for?" she asked, innocently enough.

"I'm in week two of four, staying in the hotel," he replied, indicating the building above them with a flick of his head.

She nodded slowly. "Do you get a discount at the hotel for staying for a month?"

"Oh no, I'm not staying at the hotel," he started. Then realising how contradictory that sounded, as a look of confusion flicked across Rachel's face, he explained. "A guy that I know bought one of the big rooms from the hotel. So you get to use the hotel amenities and a discount at the restaurant, that sort of thing, but you can't get room service. He's letting me stay there for a month."

"So it's a room in the hotel but it's like an apartment?" She looked surprised. "Haven't heard of that before. Nice friend for letting you stay there though."

"Oh, he's more of an acquaintance I think," he started. At her frown, he tried again. "OK, so I work—worked—for a financial services company in London. Financial Crime. Forensic Analytics." She started to ask a question but he held up a hand to stay her comment. "It's like CSI but with less blood. It's using data to investigate financial crime. Anyway, I was doing an investigation into money trafficking and came across a dodgy accountant who was moving funds through his clients' bank accounts to legitimise them. Fake invoices and receipts, and always netting out to zero so the clients never noticed."

"I'm an accountant, I think I know what Financial Crime is. Wouldn't the clients notice the transactions on their bank statements?"

"That was the beauty of it! He'd arrange for the bank accounts to be set up himself and say that the statements weren't required. He'd get himself on the company register as a Director so he could act for the company. All above board."

"Wouldn't whoever was doing the accounts at the company notice?"

"Again, he was ingenious. He'd only do this with the less sophisticated clients, the ones where his accountancy firm were doing most things, all the monthly invoices, all the VAT, all the work. So nobody noticed."

"So you found all this out and told your friend and he gave you a month in his hotel room?"

"Not quite. So you know HMRC in the UK? Like the IRD here and the IRS in the US. The tax people. So the HMRC takes a hard line on money trafficking, and they don't believe people when they say, 'It was my accountant'. In fact, they think that anyone in that situation is taking the proverbial and they go after them big time. Ignorance is not a defence. So you had fifty business owners looking at jail time and significant fines because they'd been more focused on running their hair salon or Airbnb, rather than following what their trusted accountant had been doing. We dealt with HMRC a lot, so had a relationship with one of the guys there. We had an off-the-record conversation with him and let him know that these guys were innocent. They came back and said that they'd still pursue them. I didn't think that was on, so I leaked a few of the transcripts and data points to the business owners—ones that would keep them out of jail should the HMRC keep pursuing them. I tried to do it anonymously, but this guy Reggie tracked me down and insisted on thanking me with the hotel stay. I protested because of how it looked. You can't go around accepting gifts like this. But by then I had left the firm and he explained that he was changing Airbnb management companies, so his apartment would be empty and unrentable for a month, and therefore no financial benefit."

Rachel didn't say anything, looking thoughtful.

"Usually at this point, people that I tell that story to say something like, 'That sounds really unfair, surely the HMRC aren't like that!'" continued Mike.

Rachel smiled. "Maya and I work for the same accountancy firm. It's not too much different from the IRD."

It was Mike's turn to smile. "Not the same firm our beau over there works for too? Do I need to tell HR about an interoffice relationship?"

Rachel laughed. "You're funny! No, different firms. Back to your story.

11

That was a nice thing that you did. Did you get in trouble for it?"

Mike's smile faded. "No, I never did find out how Reg tracked me down, but me leaving my firm was unrelated to that engagement." Mike noticed that Rachel was looking over his shoulder and turned to see Maya sitting alone, staring daggers at Rachel. The guy she was with came out of the bathrooms and headed towards them.

"Another Stella and a glass of house white, please," he said to Jim.

"How's the date going?" Mike asked him.

He looked surprised that Mike knew he was on a date. "Oh, OK I guess," he allowed, paying for the drinks with a card and then heading back after a curious glance at the trio of Jim, Rachel and Mike. Maya shot one last meaningful look at Rachel before turning her attention to her drink and her date.

"You're in trouble, you're in trouble!" sang Mike quietly, waggling his finger childishly.

Rachel laughed, enjoying herself. "So you just stay in your room during the day and hang out here at night? It doesn't sound like you're really seeing much of New Zealand. Don't you have pubs in London?"

"Haha, we certainly do have pubs in England. My place is actually in a commuter town outside of London. I might have painted a bleak picture of my time here so far but Jim has given me some good pointers. Last week I did some day trips: Devonport, Waiheke Island and Hobbiton, and I spent the weekend down in Queenstown. So I've tried to get out and about. But when I'm in the room, I read or watch TV and use the sauna, Jacuzzis and pools. Go for a workout in the gym. When I get bored I come down and shoot the breeze with Jim here—and occasionally make a new friend."

Behind them, the conversation between Maya and her date had become heated and voices were becoming raised. It was impossible not to hear the conversation now—the protesting of innocence on one side and the anger on the other. The decibels rose accordingly until Maya scooped up her jacket

12

and flounced out with a meaningful look at Rachel and a snort in the direction of the men in the pub.

"I should go," began Rachel. "Are you going to be around the rest of the week?"

"I should be here," agreed Mike. "Goodnight!"

She left with a smile over one shoulder, pulling on her puffer as she went. The guy was left at his seat in the booth, frowning and shaking his head as he finished his drink. A few minutes later he too pulled his jacket on and headed out into the rain, looking intently at his phone.

"Well, that was exciting!" said Mike. "I wonder what he said that pissed her off so much."

Jim gave him a look. "He obviously asked if she wanted to go back to his place. Or hers. They looked to be getting on OK, so maybe if he'd waited for the second or third date she might have said yes, but..."

"Oh! And her friend was there, so Rachel would know if she went home with him!"

"Yeah, it did seem like a major overreaction. Might have been just for show."

Mike studied Jim. "I guess you've seen it all, right? Being a barman you see all sorts of interactions—it's like getting a psychology degree."

"I'll take your word for that. I didn't even finish high school."

"Hmmm...." said Mike, lost in thought.

"Rachel seemed to like you. Do you think she'll pop by tomorrow?"

Mike grinned. "Maybe. She seemed OK."

The next day dragged. He'd had maybe half a beer too many, just enough to give him the start of a headache. A brisk run on the treadmill followed by an invigorating swim in the outdoor pool after breakfast cleared his head. He dried himself poolside and put his robe and slippers on before returning to his room. The corridors were empty of the trays and he idly wondered what time they cleared them. He did know that room service for breakfast was based on a door hanger—a cardboard checkbox list of breakfast items where you could indicate which things you wanted and then hang it on the door handle. As long as you got it on the door handle by 3am they'd satisfy the requirements. He guessed that there would be some staff member who would patrol the hallways at 3:05am clearing the leftover dinner trays and collecting the breakfast orders. Fun job.

That evening he returned to the pub. Jim smiled when he walked in. Mike had made a little more of an effort with his appearance, shaving and selecting a dress shirt with vest and blazer over his normal jeans. He may have even added product to his hair. He considered finding a barber to give his fade a touch up but he didn't know anywhere suitable in Auckland. But it was in vain, as Rachel did not come in. Still, Jim was always good company and they chatted about this and that, dwelling a little on the weekend when Jim worked security instead of behind the bar—always an entertaining experience hearing about the shenanigans drunken people got up to. As a result of the conversations and how much he'd had to drink the night before, Mike drank less and headed back to his room at a reasonable hour.

It must have been about 9pm by the time the lift pinged, announcing his presence and depositing him on his floor. The corridors were populated as usual by the remnants of room service and, as he made his way up the middle of the corridor, he noticed an almost-complete burger with bacon peeking out from under a napkin, only a couple of bites taken from it. He hadn't eaten dinner before heading down to the pub, expecting to meet Rachel and maybe have a drink or two before inviting her out to eat somewhere, playing the "I'm a tourist where would you recommend eating?" card. He looked longingly at the burger but wasn't desperate enough or drunk enough to pause and give it any more attention. But as he turned the corner to head towards his room, the corridor he'd just walked along became fully visible out of the corner of his eye. He took three steps along the new length of corridor before his eye convinced his brain of what he'd just seen. Or thought he'd seen.

A man, a slim man, short, with straggly hair and a beard, dressed in jean shorts and a robe, crouched over the tray with the burger. Mike paused, wondering if he was imagining things. Perhaps the image in his head was a throwback to a movie he'd seen while half asleep or drunk. Nope. Nothing came to mind. He had to check, so reversed the three steps and turned to face the corridor.

Empty. Obviously imagining things.

He headed onwards to his room, ignoring the twin voices in his head, one whispering, "Check if the burger is there, you saw a man!" and the competing one which whispered, "Check if the burger is there, eat it!" When he got to his room, he placed a pie in the microwave, flicked on the TV and watched a bit of late-night comedy. Even covered in tomato sauce the pie was a poor substitute for the corridor burger, and by the time he went to bed he'd almost convinced himself that what he'd seen was the result of an overactive imagination.

The next day was an unusual one. Instead of wind and rain, or cloud and rain, the day dawned bright and clear. And still. No wind at all. Jim had told him about the bike rental system in the city, so he downloaded the app and checked out where the nearest bike was. Rather than having parking stations like the 'Boris bikes' in London, each bike was left where it was and a GPS system tracked it. Carrying a light waterproof jacket just in case it rained, Mike set off.

The first bike he found was leaning against an apartment building nearby. It turned out to be missing a saddle. The next one was a five-minute walk away, but this one was missing a pedal. The third one was missing both pedals. Each was about a five to ten-minute walk from the other and as he strolled across the city from disabled bike to disabled bike, he thought to himself that he was at least getting a nice walk in the sun. The next bike was missing a back wheel. The one after that was only missing the footrest of the pedal. The central metal pin was still there. That would make things tricky, but at least he would be able to ride instead of walking. But he wanted to enjoy the ride, so he headed on to the next location. Someone had managed to get a bike high up on top of a street light. It hung there, precariously balanced on top of the candy cane curve. Mike was tempted to shake the street light and try to dislodge it, but the dangling chain dissuaded him from that exercise.

The next GPS location was slightly off the main footpath—some bushes beneath a motorway overpass. This bike was quite impressive. Both wheels were missing. The next one looked like it could be a winner though. Two wheels, two pedals, a seat, handlebars—everything seemed to be in place, until he realised as he pedalled maniacally to no effect that it didn't have a chain at all.

He gave up. There was a bike rental place near the waterfront so he headed down the hill through the CBD to see how much they charged. As he approached the store he noticed a seemingly complete bike in the same colours as the ones on the app. A quick check of the app indicated that this was an available bike. And a closer physical inspection indicated that it was in fact rideable. He activated the bike on the app and heard the audible clunk as the bike's locking system disengaged and allowed him to ride gingerly away. He was waiting for a pedal to fall off, the chain to break, or something in general to happen to make the bike unrideable. But nothing untoward happened.

The bike path wound through the central city, passing the port on the left. Mike cycled along for a while, watching the cranes moving containers from stacks on the wharves to waiting trucks on the other side of a red railing fence. A little way along, the road left the city centre and the ports behind. There was a rescue helicopter landing pad on the left and some sort of lake on the right. The lake seemed to have a public swimming pool beside it.

Must be lovely when it's warm, thought Mike. The sun was bright and held the memory of summer heat, unlike the pale midwinter sun that he was used to in England. He passed a marina and crossed a bridge where two Asian men were fishing. By now the bike path was not an afterthought splitting the space of the single footpath, but a full-sized partner. On the other side of the road, it was the same, but with a better brown surface, with additional grip.

On the right, a basin was bordered by a mini-golf course and then a yacht club, but Mike was content to cruise along, looking out over the harbour. The view on his left was out to Devonport on the North Shore, and beyond that to the volcanic triangle of Rangitoto. As he left the yacht club behind him, the road started to rise until he noticed that they were going over another bridge. Looking back the way he'd come, he could see the skyscrapers of the city poking above a line of trees and headlands. In the distance, the cranes of the port looked like misplaced parts of a bridge.

He spent another hour cycling around bays and beaches. The white sand beaches were surrounded by a small collection of shops and restaurants. There was no surf, just an expanse of slightly shelly sand leading out to the gently lapping sea. The hills behind the bays were dotted with the houses of the well-to-do, surrounded by ample vegetation. By the time he'd run out of the flat beachside bike track (the path continued onwards but at a steepness he wasn't keen on), he was ready for some food. So he stopped in St Heliers at a fish and chip shop and took his fish supper to the beach and ate it on the sand. They didn't have vinegar for his chips, so he had to content himself with a desultory squirt of tomato sauce. They'd looked at him strangely when he'd asked for brown sauce as well. Philistines!

Sunlight glinted off the waves in the harbour. Yummy mummies in Lycra collected coffees, some pushing prams with rugged up children aboard, some congregating in couples and trios. Mike was about halfway through his lunch when a swarm of seagulls noticed him and descended, screeching and demanding chips. He kept them at bay by waving his foot periodically, sending the closest two or three flapping briefly before they resumed their positions. It was harder to enjoy the view and meal while being watched by so many beady little eyes, so after a few more bites, Mike took the remains to the rubbish bin and dumped what was left inside before returning to the bike track for the return journey.

The trip back was uneventful. He took the shore-side of the road, even though that caused interruptions as various roads led away from the waterfront. Even so, the other side had a consistent flow of joggers, cyclists and pedestrians, which meant he made better progress with less traffic on his side. When he reached the city he was in two minds. There were no cycle paths and he didn't feel confident enough to ride on the road, so he elected to ride on the wide footpaths, heading up the main shopping street before turning up the side street that led up to the hotel. The hill was quite steep, so eventually he decided to take out his phone, log onto the app and end his hire session, hearing the clunk as the locking mechanism re-engaged.

Feeling like he'd achieved something for the day, he headed back into the hotel and checked his emails, then fell into a YouTube rabbit hole that veered from historic battles in the Crimean War to the Tower of Babel and the Yellow Horde. The light outside started to fail around 5:30pm, and by 6:30pm the city was in full darkness. Mike was used to England where in midwinter it got darker much earlier as it was ten degrees or so further from the equator. This meant that he was a little shocked it was so late when he looked up from his YouTubing, expecting it to be a couple of hours earlier. He freshened up with a quick shower and threw on a fresh dress shirt before heading down to the pub, just in case Rachel turned up.

THE DATE

It was a surprise to see another patron in the pub mid-week, and a joyful one when he registered that it was none other than Rachel chatting amicably with Jim.

"Wonderful to see you again, Rachel! How's Maya? How're you, Jim?"

Jim smiled, nodded back and started pouring him his usual.

Rachel gave a wry grin. "She's giving up on men, she says."

"Tell her I respect her life decision," grinned back Mike. "What are you drinking?"

"Oh, I was just about to get a vodka, lime and lemonade."

Mike nodded to Jim and he set Mike's lager on the bar and started on Rachel's drink. Rachel had her hair arranged in a tight low bun and was wearing a black square-cut dress. "I like your hair," he said while they waited. "Is that a French plait?"

She grinned. "No, it's just a bun. But thank you." She nodded her thanks to Jim when he finished her drink. "I'll get the next one," she said, raising it in a toast. "To new friends."

Mike was quick to follow suit. "New friends."

"So what did you get up to today? I was staring out the window all day at the sun. Please tell me that you managed to get outside?"

Mike smiled. "I learnt a new word." He mentioned the name of the rental bike firm. "You may think it means to go for a bike ride, but in fact it means an hour-long walk trying to find a bike that works."

Jim and Rachel dutifully laughed.

"But I did find one eventually and rode down to St Heliers and had fish and chips by the beach."

"Ah, St Heliers, that is a lovely route. You get to see the nice part of the city. The views across the harbour are great."

"Yeah, I got to see some of the other places I've been from a different angle. Devonport and Waiheke Island."

"So what has your favourite place been so far?"

"I liked Queenstown, and Hobbiton was a hoot. I loved the hobbit houses, it's a pity you can't go inside."

"And do you like New Zealand?"

Mike laughed out loud. "Sorry," he said at her shocked look. "When I arrived I'd just got off the plane and got into a taxi to come to the hotel, and when I told the driver the address, he noticed my accent and the first thing he asked was 'How do you like New Zealand?' It was tempting to say, 'Well the airport is OK, but that's all I've seen of it so far'. And now you're keen on finding out what I think too. Two data points make a trend. So why are Kiwis so desperate to find out what others think of them?"

"When you find out someone isn't from England, don't you ask them what they think of the place?"

"Yes, but we don't really care. We're just being polite. But here, it seems if you don't immediately launch into a rave about the beauty of the place then you're committing some sort of a crime."

"Hmph! I don't think that's the case at all."

"Fine, OK. I'm sure it's not. After all, it's only two data points, right? What about you, have you done much travel?"

"I have, I've been to Australia a few times." She raised a finger per city. "Sydney, Melbourne and the Gold Coast." And lowered them one by one. "Sightseeing, shopping and the beach. What about you?"

"Wow, yeah. I don't really count all the places I've been because most of them are just for work. As I said that other night, just airport, taxi, hotel, office. Not much sightseeing at all. But I've managed to get around a few European cities over the years. Berlin, Barcelona, Budapest..."

"Any place not beginning with 'B'?" asked Jim.

"Don't you have some glasses to wash or some beer to water down?" Mike asked. "As I was saying... uh... Prague - that's pretty. A great old town, medieval bridge, castle. Very bohemian. Cheap beer."

Rachel looked down at the stools that they were sitting on. "Hey, do you want to grab a booth? The seats there are a little more comfortable than these."

"Sure," said Mike. As they collected their drinks and jackets, he shrugged at Jim to show it wasn't his doing. "Thanks for that," Mike said to Rachel as he sat down. "I didn't want to be rude to Jim, but I definitely wanted to speak more... one on one."

She smiled warmly. "So tell me everything. You're what, 32?"

Mike had heard that Kiwis were unreserved, so he shouldn't have been surprised by such questions, but he was still figuring out what was within bounds for acceptable conversation, and whether it cut both ways. "Yeah, close enough. Thirty-four, unmarried, no kids, house in Buckinghamshire—that's northwest of London. About to start a new job in a couple of months."

"Buckinghamshire? Is that near Buckingham Palace?"

"No, not really, the Palace is in the middle of London. The—Duke? Earl? Baron?—of Buckingham also owned the Palace and so gave it his name."

"Any family? Brothers? Sisters?"

"No, my mother died having me. Dad passed away a few years ago. I have an Aunt that I've grown apart from who lives in Finsbury Park. But nope, an only son, no siblings."

"Oh, I am so sorry about your mother."

"But not my father?"

21

The look of panic on her face was priceless, and he felt a little mean. "I'm sorry—I'm kidding, I'm kidding. I was brought up by my grandparents with my Dad. Of course, I miss what could have been, but they all came to my graduation and were very proud of me and what I'd become, so I was very lucky. I keep them with me always," he tapped the centre of his suit jacket.

"In your heart," Rachel said, nodding.

"No, their photos are in my wallet," he said, pulling it out and showing it to her.

She watched him wryly. "You know, you have a very... peculiar sense of humour."

"I am who I am, no question. But what about you? Family?"

"Both parents are still alive. Mum's just turned fifty and Dad's a year older. I'm the eldest of four, so a large family."

"And do you get along with all your siblings?"

She sighed. "Sure... though it gets to the stage where you change but their perception of you stays the same. And they think they know the real you, because, hey, they lived with you for twenty years, right? They saw you develop and grow into the person you've become, but then nothing after that. That's who they think you are. Never mind the years after that, right? They'll never let you forget the time you backed the car into the fence, or the time that you got drunk and came through the neighbours' ceiling. Or the time you got drunk and threw up in the washing machine instead of the toilet and then went to sleep without telling anyone."

"Sounds like some great stories. Tell me more about those."

Rachel's eyes widened as she realized she wasn't painting herself in the best light. "My teen years were a little rebellious."

Mike smiled at her discomfort before letting her off the hook. "Yeah, my Aunt was a bit like that too. She'd say, 'I remember the time you took off your nappy and ran around the room naked.' Comments they think should endear them to you with reference to how long they've known you, but all it does is make you think that they're trying to embarrass you."

"So were you very rebellious?"

"In my youth? My friends in high school got into a few scrapes, but the more adventurous they got, the less I hung out with them. By the time I was ready for university, I was a bit of a loner. At graduation, it was the four of us in the local pub having a half of lager."

"You, your dad and grandparents?"

"Yes. And then when you're working such long hours in Audit, the only people you really get to know are your colleagues. And then after that in Forensics, you're out on a client site for long periods. The client looks at you with suspicion or hate, so it's a bit of a lonely existence. There I go— making myself sound like some sort of a pariah! I'm sociable! I party!"

"Oh, when was the last time you got absolutely shit-faced?"

"I must admit, it's been a while. Probably at one of my colleague's leaving drinks. Call it three months ago. They were rolling off the project I was on and leaving the firm as well, so we managed to get the leaving party put on the project code—£1,500 on food and booze. That's about $3,000 in your local currency!"

"Sounds like a lot, but how many people was that for?"

"That was just for ten of us."

She whistled. "That's a pretty good night!"

"It was, it was. What about you? Any late-night shenanigans when it's the busy season after year end?"

"No, nothing like that. Me and Maya are still juniors, so we work late but we don't party or anything. I guess you put all that behind you after university, right?"

"You don't have to, but isn't that part of maturing and growing up? No more laundry loads smelling of vomit?"

"Yeah, but... this is going to sound sad, but... is that what we sold ourselves out for? We traded getting drunk or stoned, and acting a little silly, for a bit of financial security and social acceptability? What about our freedom? Fun? Maybe I should have done my O.E."

"Sorry, your... ?"

"O.E. Overseas Experience. It's a Kiwi rite of passage. You go to university, graduate, go overseas for two years—usually to the UK—and work in bars over there. Do some travel on the Continent and then come back to New Zealand with a damaged liver, a swollen credit card bill and a hazy memory of the must-see spots in Europe to start your professional life with all of your wild oats sown. Although most people I hear about can only get bar work, can't afford to go travelling so come back home with the liver damage, the credit card debt and a hazy memory of dossing in shared accommodation with ten other Antipodeans for two years with cold damp winters. I decided I'd rather have a two-year head start on the career, thank you very much. But one or two of my fellow students got work in accountancy over there, so they came back after two years smiling. They had enough money from their accountancy jobs to do the travel, and live comfortably, some of them even managing to save and take advantage of the exchange rate. Plus, their overseas accountancy experience was looked upon favourably here, so they're ahead of me in the pecking order at work. Let's just say I'm in two minds on whether I did the right thing."

"Still, you can't go back, right? Oh, you've finished your drink, let me get another."

"No—sit down. I can get the next round. You're going to have to learn something about Kiwi women, Mike—we don't need no man to buy us our drinks."

He beckoned to Jim who wasted no time coming over.

"Rachel's buying, so can I get a glass of your finest scotch? Just kidding, same again, thanks."

"Same again thanks Jim," added Rachel, before prodding Mike in the chest. Jim brought them over almost straight away, making Mike wonder if he'd prepared them as he saw them getting close to empty.

"You are a big tease—you're like my brother, always trying to get a rise out of me."

Mike looked sheepish. "So, tell me, do all Kiwis do this 'O.E.'?"

Rachel looked confused. "All my friends did it."

"I mean, what about people who didn't go to university? What if they did a trade qualification? Or if they didn't finish high school? Do they go overseas for two years?"

"Oh! Uh... I guess not. It's really expensive to travel from New Zealand, so if the governments didn't have a special arrangement to let us work there, I don't think we would have gone."

"I guess it's a little like a 'gap yah'."

"A what now?"

"Sorry, a 'gap year'. A year-long gap in education between high school and university. I call it 'gap yah' because that's how the posh people pronounce it. And it's usually only the posh people who can afford it. Sometimes they do charity work in the developing world, sometimes it's an unpaid internship somewhere that Daddy's arranged. But, yeah, great for them. I went straight to uni on a part scholarship, but I still had to work pretty hard to pay the bills and study. No gap yah for me."

"A self-made man in more ways than one, I like it."

They continued chatting until Rachel finished her drink.

"Hey Mike, I've actually got to run, but would you like to ask me out for dinner tomorrow?"

"Sure." He waited a humorous beat. "Hey Rachel, would you like to go out for dinner tomorrow night? Say 7pm?"

"Ooh... I'll have to check my diary. That sounds wonderful, I'd love to. Meet you here?"

"Sure! That sounds perfect."

And just like that she picked up her jacket and stood up, kissed him on the cheek, her hand lingering a little long on his bicep, and then she was out the door into the cold. Mike blinked at the abruptness of her departure and took his drink to finish it at the bar.

Jim grinned at him as he sat down. "How did that go?"

Mike thought for a moment. "OK, I guess. She left kind of sudden though. Don't quite know what to make of that."

"Are you seeing her again?"

"Yeah, tomorrow night. I guess that's a good sign."

Close to 24 hours later he had the chance to find out what had caused the abrupt abandonment of the first date. He'd spent the day watching the rain come in from the harbour, sheets of it bombarding the city. The view of the car park building next door was actually quite entertaining. The lower floors filled up quickly, leaving the open roof as the only place for casual parkers to use. The wind gusted evilly, making the mad dash from the car to the lifts or stairs particularly harrowing. Those parking their cars had to choose between being dry under their umbrellas but potentially losing the umbrella to one or other of the violent gusts, or else accept that they would get wet and make the mad dash across the exposed rooftop to the lift, the puddles and painted lines on the floor making the footing treacherous. It was another day spent on the internet or staring at the rain, watching movies and otherwise blobbing out. Even the visit to the gym was a bit ho-hum. Just for laughs he went for a swim for a few laps in the rain before shivering across the small distance to the Jacuzzi to warm back up. It was no wonder that he had the facilities to himself.

Rachel walked in at 7 sharp, greeting Jim by name and repeating the kiss on Mike's cheek that he'd enjoyed the previous day. "Shall we go?" she asked.

"Don't wait up," Mike told Jim with a wink. Jim returned to drying a glass with a cloth and a snort.

"So where are we going?" asked Rachel when they were outside. They were protected from the rain by the awning over the footpath, but the wind was still gusting and the rain had only slightly eased off to showers, so Mike didn't really want to go too far away. He knew there was a Denny's on the other end of the block, so he suggested it—only semi-seriously if truth be told, so he was surprised when Rachel agreed.

They ascended the stairs to be met with a counter surrounded by various posters and warnings. As the waitress came over to take them to their table, Mike stared open-mouthed at them all. Rachel caught his expression and asked what the problem was. He said he'd tell her when they sat down. The waitress led them to a corner booth where they could see into the belly of the restaurant, the comfortable padding of the seats starting to look a little threadbare. "So what caused the shock at the entrance?"

"Did you see all the warnings? Think about it—every warning sign has a story? A reason for it being there, an incident after which management decided, no more! We need a sign to stop this from happening again. And you saw them all up there—we will ask for your money if you go outside for a smoke. Sounds like a few dine and dashers. All assaults reported to police. No brainer there."

"Oh! You probably don't know—this is the place the kids come after clubbing. It's cheap, central and more importantly it's open 24/7. So there is probably nothing the night shift hasn't seen—sketchy overdoses, drunken hookups and general bad behaviour."

"Haha, so what does that say about me that I said we should come here?"

Rachel smiled, placing a cross on an imaginary clipboard. "Points off there, true."

"So did I get too many points off last night? You kind of ran off in a hurry."

Rachel was a little slow to answer, and he could almost see the inner argument raging back and forwards. "So... me and Maya read this book on

27

dating, and we thought we'd try it out. One of the rules is that on the first date, you can stay for an hour or for two drinks, whichever comes first. And the time ticked over so I had to go."

"Ah... and you both follow these rules religiously, do you?"

"Well, it doesn't say anything about overseas visitors specifically...."

"Phew," said Mike.

"But anyway, what did you want to eat? She's coming back."

Mike ended up getting the burger while Rachel elected to get the pumpkin, spinach and feta lasagne.

"Are you a vegetarian?" Mike asked.

"Not really," she responded. "I just had a meaty lunch. So, tell me, what are you looking for?"

Mike eyed her quizzically over the bottles of condiments. "Are all Kiwi girls as... upfront as you are?"

"No point beating around the bush, is there?" she said, not taking offence. "It lets us know if we're on the same page."

"I guess... OK... well, I suppose I'm looking to find someone who wants the same things that I do and has the same values. That's not terribly helpful, is it? How many people say that they're looking for someone who is the exact opposite of them or want to be challenged at every turn by a different set of values?"

Rachel smiled encouragingly. Mike wondered if the book she'd read had a script or whether there really was a checklist.

"See, my least favourite part of dating is the inevitable Vietnam Reaction."

"The what?"

"OK, bear with me. The Americans, before they went into Vietnam, had fought the Nazis in World War Two. Two large standing armies going head to head. And so that was the thinking when they went into Vietnam—they were fighting their last war. You go into the next battle with the same

THE MAN IN THE HOTEL CEILING

mindset which won you the previous war, right? Don't mess with success. But of course Vietnam was different—a guerrilla war, so things didn't go as well."

"OK....? Oh, thanks," Rachel said as their food arrived.

"Now in the dating world, you get the same thing,' continued Mike. "You focus too much on the deal breakers of the previous partners. 'She was too controlling,' so I'll look for someone who isn't controlling. But while you're focused so intently on whether this new person is a control freak, you miss the fact that this new person is totally irresponsible with time or money or both. Then, after her, you're totally overly sensitive to people who are late. You're always fighting the last war—the Vietnam Reaction. But, in answer to your question, of course I'm looking for that forever person, someone who I feel comfortable with and get along with and can hang out with."

"Even on the other side of the world?"

"Of course!"

They were quiet for a little while, concentrating on eating. 'How is it?' asked Mike. "It needs meat, doesn't it?"

A little later, after a curiously deflating conversation balloon about splitting the bill, Rachel walked Mike back to the hotel foyer.

"Can we be honest with each other, Mike?"

I've been nothing but honest, Rachel, thought Mike. But merely nodded.

"I don't really want to move overseas. My life is here—my family, my friends, my job. Normally I would take you home anyway and we'd make sweet, sweet love, and then I'd cry for days after you went back to the UK because even though two weeks is not really enough time to fall in love and have you stay here in New Zealand, I'd still be expecting that because, you know, movies. And that book says that you're better off not having one night stands because it clouds your thinking for when a possible partner does come along. They say, 'Sometimes it's better to forego the night of passion to keep yourself ready for the relationship when it does come along'. So, I'm going to be good and head home now."

"OK. Well, I think that's a bit of a pity, because I've had fun these last two nights, but I respect your wishes." No matter the bogus reasoning, he thought a little wryly. She gave him the usual kiss on the cheek and headed back into the cold Auckland night.

Despite how they'd left it, Mike was dissatisfied with how things had ended with Rachel. He was replaying the conversation in his mind, trying to see how he could have arrived at a different outcome from the evening, when he decided on a whim to walk up the stairs instead of taking the lift. He climbed them slowly, lost in thought with scenarios flicking through his head. He reached his floor and headed out past the lifts into the corridor that led back to his room. Ahead of him, about midway along the corridor, a slim figure was collecting food from a tray and walking away from him. The person hadn't seen him, and moved quickly with darting movements down the corridor to the corner at the end. Here they turned right instead of left, opened a service door and disappeared from sight. As soon as the door swung closed, Mike ran after them. He reached the door as it clicked shut and tried to open it. It swung open, revealing a short corridor, devoid of decoration and looking exactly like the one he'd just left except without any room doors. The corridor ended in a service lift with yellow tape crossing the doors in an X. Even if the lift had been waiting for the person he was chasing, Mike should have been able to see the doors closing—this corridor was short. He thought for a second.

There were no trapdoors in the floor, no doors in the walls and presumably, if the lift didn't work, then he obviously couldn't have caught it. That left just the ceiling. Directly above him was a hatch in the ceiling.

And now that he thought about it, there was a slight smudge on the wall above the textured skirting board about waist high. But how would you get to the ceiling from there? The man he'd seen was short, so he couldn't have launched from the skirting board and pulled himself through the ceiling hatch, could he?

Just for fun, Mike jumped up to see if he could at least touch the ceiling hatch. He came up short. Really short. Shaking his head as he tried to figure it out, he headed back to his room. He had definitely seen the man. That was certain now. Someone was living in the ceiling of the hotel, feeding on leftover room service meals. By the time he reached his room, he'd decided a couple of things. The first was that he wouldn't mention the man to anyone. Not directly anyway. But all of a sudden he had something to focus on for the remaining two weeks. It was like a forensic engagement—pull together as much data as you can to try and figure out the central question. Who was the man in the hotel ceiling?

THE BREAK-IN

"How are you finding the room?" Jim asked, leaning against the back of the bar.

"It's great," replied Mike, "but there's like three big-screen TVs, so I don't know what that's about. Who needs two big-screen TVs beside each other in the lounge and another one in the bedroom?"

"Maybe it's one of those magic eye things. If you stand at the right place it'll look like 3D?"

"Maybe," snorted Mike.

"You haven't found any bullet holes?" Jim asked casually, closely watching Mike.

"Bullet holes?"

"You hadn't heard? About a month before you arrived there was some sort of gunfight in one of the rooms. They tried to hush it up but Greg, the owner of the bar, was accepting deliveries when he saw the cops turn up. So he went out later on to have a cigarette with some of the kitchen staff and found out one of the guests had been gunned down in their doorway. The hotel kept it quiet—it was people that owned rather than a guest in a hotel room, but you don't want that sort of thing to get out. It would affect bookings, right?"

"I had no idea. Was it a robbery?"

"Apparently, nothing was taken. The room service guy found the door open and the guy lying in a pool of his own blood. They originally thought that his husband did it because he's been missing since it happened, but the angle of the body and the fact he was blocking the door from closing, means whoever shot him was outside the front door."

"Do you know what room number that was? Did the press pick it up?"

"Can't help you with that, sorry."

"Wow, do you know the guy's name at least?"

"Sorry, Mike, I've told you all that I know. I mean, I could make something up, but it wouldn't be true. You'll just have to investigate it yourself, right?"

Mike made a face. "I'm supposed to be on holiday! But you're right. It's quite the conundrum." He got up.

"You going so soon?" asked Jim.

"The mystery is eating at me," admitted Mike, pushing his barstool in. "I'll catch you tomorrow?"

"Latin Dancing, remember?" reminded Jim.

"Ah yeah—maybe after the weekend then? Do you guys do Sunday roasts?"

"Best to come before 6pm, the cook goes home then and we just reheat the leftovers."

Mike headed back to his room, the news of the killing colliding with what he knew of the man in the ceiling. It was quite obvious what had happened—someone was hiding from an assassin—but the why's were starting to accumulate. Why had the guy been shot? Why hadn't the husband gone to the police?

He sat down in front of his laptop and pondered. There should be an apartment owners group of some sort and hopefully they would have an online presence. Maybe a list of members, with their room numbers. With that he should be able to do a social media search to find the life story of the poor unfortunates who had lived in that particular apartment. Depending on the security settings, he might be able to see all their photos and their friends and paint a picture of who they were and how they lived their lives. Maybe even get some leads to follow up with some questions. If they were professionals and on professional networking sites, he should be able to fill the gaps in terms of their jobs and likely salaries, and maybe get leads to people who worked with them. He got to work.

It turned out there were a lot of owners in the building. He had a list of the room numbers and their names but most just had initials, so there were no obvious clues like "Joseph and Frank Smith", and so no way to go through each of their social media accounts. He needed some way of narrowing down the list. Maybe a quick look at each of the doors would give some sort of clue? He wrote down all the room numbers and headed out.

He started with the rooms on his floor. The first couple of doors looked like... doors. No discerning marks or other evidence of gunshots. But the last room on his floor paid off. The door jamb had sections that showed fresh paint, the area above the doorway in particular showing a colour-mismatched line of dots rising up until they hit the ceiling. He was too far away from them to be able to tell much more than that, so he pulled out his phone and took some photos, zooming in on the bullet holes for some photos and making sure he got some with the door jamb and the lowest of the bullet holes close up. He headed back to his room with a bounce in his step. Things were coming together.

He looked up the names on the ownership records. G D and G H Steptoe. The G D turned out to be Gary Darren and the G H was Gavin Harold. Social media accounts were locked down, so that was a dead-end, but at least he had confirmation of their names. A half-hour on Google returned some athletic records and photos and confirmed their rough ages, while a search in the death notices indicated that Gary had died suddenly of 'natural causes' and been cremated last month. Mike frowned at that. Sure, it would be natural for someone to die if introduced to lead flying at speed in the form of bullets fired from a gun, but that reeked of a cover-up. In lieu of flowers, the death notice asked that donations be made in his name to the local hospice. The athletic photos showed Gary and Gavin running—they both had a slight build and they were on the shorter side, so when they were in the same photo they looked good together, but as soon as you saw them with other people they looked like a pair of hobbits in the Lord of the Rings movies. They were very much alike. Both in their early thirties and, according to LinkedIn, Gary worked in international banking at one of the local banks. Mike couldn't find anything on Gavin on LinkedIn, so assumed that he didn't have a professional career. This turned out to be true. When he searched using his full name it came up with a website promoting Gavin as a freelance writer and editor.

Mike was starting to piece together the pieces of the story. Gary's role at the bank was an obvious clue. Someone in organised crime was blackmailing Gary into moving money internationally and he had refused, leading to him getting shot on his doorstep. He couldn't figure out why Gavin had disappeared, but if that wasn't it, maybe there was some sort of smuggling of illicit goods and the import papers were sitting with Gary and the organised crime syndicate needed them to get the goods off the wharf. Either way, all Mike had to do was find a way to talk with Gavin and boom, case solved. A quick visit to the local police force, a pause for some photos of him shaking hands with the police chief and he had a nice little line for his CV.

He thought he'd do a bit of due diligence with the hotel staff and headed down to the front desk. A pair of uniformed personnel attended to a small group of guests checking in. One was a tall and sickly thin youth in his early twenties with a wispy suggestion of a moustache and a pair of black glass beads pierced in one ear. The edges of a tattoo peeked out from under the collar of his shirt. His colleague was a chipper young lady of similar age who was all earnest concentration. She was serving the group checking in while he studiously looked at the computer screen on the desk.

"Hi, uh, Adam, is it? Hi, I'm in room 410 and I've got a question about the corridor on the fourth floor."

"Hi, sir, I'll be with you in just a second, just looking something up here..." And then after a pause. "Ah, OK, sir, sorry, how can I help?"

"So I've got a question about that side corridor on the fourth floor—the one with a service lift?"

Adam was the master of the pregnant pause. "Oh yeah, the service lift has been out of action for a little while now. Man, it's taking a while. We're waiting on a part to be shipped over from Germany, so it's going to be out of action for a bit longer yet. It's cool, there's no impact to any of our services—room service delivery comes up in the main lift now. Is there anything else I can help you with?"

Adam's colleague—Sharon, according to her name badge—had finished up with the group of guests and turned to listen to the conversation.

Mike tried a different topic. "So what can you tell me about room 417?" he asked, referring to Gavin and Gary's room.

Adam froze and Mike glanced at Sharon. Her eyes grew wide and she physically moved to place herself more between Mike and Adam. "I'm sorry sir, all media enquiries need to go through our head office press team. We're not at liberty to talk about room 417 or the break-in to the utilities closet."

"Ah, cool, thanks for that. I'll do that, cheers," Mike said as he backed away. He started to head back to his room before a thought occurred to him, and he braved the cold and nipped around the corner to the pub.

Jim was sitting at a stool behind the bar. A couple in the corner booth were staring into each other's eyes and talking quietly. Jim raised his eyebrows in greeting and indicated the couple with a tilt of his head. "Much less exciting, those two," he said, referring to the explosive way Maya had left the pub at the end of her date.

Mike grinned. "Got a weird question for you. What utilities are accessed through the hotel's utility closet?"

Jim shrugged. "I don't know, utilities maybe? Why?"

Mike winked. "I can't tell you. But if you can find out for me that would be cool. You mentioned that the owner found out about the shooting from the staff, so anything you can find out would be awesome."

Jim looked at him for a moment, frowning slightly. "Hmmm... OK, I guess I can see what I can find out. But you owe me one. Hey, how did it go with Rachel?"

Mike winced. "I'm going back to England soon, and she's not looking to be just a holiday romance. Which is a pity, because she's a cool chick."

Jim nodded. "Yeah, she seemed to be into you too. A pity. I guess you've got a life back in England, friends and family and a job to go back for, right?"

Mike smiled. "Something like that. Listen I hate to be rude, but I've got to go—please do let me know if you find out anything."

Jim nodded. "Sure, will do."

THE MEETING

The best idea Mike could come up with that wouldn't spook Gavin was to write a little note and leave it near the ceiling hatch. Anything else seemed too intrusive. He ruled out getting a ladder and climbing up into the hatch. If Gavin was afraid for his life, and his husband had already been assassinated, then it was likely he would see any unauthorised attempts to enter as potentially life-threatening, and Mike didn't want to be the victim of Gavin's attempts at self-defence. Likewise, ambushing Gavin when he came out to feed seemed to be treating him like a feral creature and that would likely put him on the back foot.

But it couldn't be an enormous poster either, in case one of the hotel staff saw it. Mike eventually settled for a bright green Post-it note, with an innocuous message on it: "Hi Gavin, would love to chat over a coffee. You can get me on +44 7626 049946, Mike Reid 410". After breakfast, he took the note and went to the service corridor. He stuck it to the wall about halfway between his head and the ceiling - high enough to be out of eye level but impossible to miss from the hatch. He figured that even if the stickiness wore off and the note floated to the ground, it would still be visible from the hatch, the lime green standing out against the carpet pattern.

He headed back to his room and thought about how he could make Gavin feel safe. And where they might have their coffee. There was a cafe in the foyer of the hotel, so maybe they could go there? A knock at the door interrupted his thoughts, and he absentmindedly went to the door and opened it. There stood Gavin.

Twenty-five years ago a friend of Mike's had gone to the vet to buy two kittens—one jet black with white marks on its paws and face, the other a mottled apricot, brown and grey. Mike had been there when the kittens had been released into their new home. They'd disappeared out of the cage in a flash and still hadn't been seen by the early evening. Mike had helped search for them, eventually tracking them down to the basement, cowering in the darkest corner, their eyes wide in terror at every bump and noise. They weren't rescue cats, just scared of all the new experiences and being overwhelmed by the new stimuli. Gavin reminded him of them.

"Uh, Mike?" Gavin croaked, holding up the Post-it.

"Oh, yes, please, do come in," said Mike, backing into the room with his hands out awkwardly, showing that they were empty. Gavin caught the door as it started to close and slid into the room. Mike concentrated on keeping his voice low and level. "I'm really glad you came," he said, getting a good look at him. For his part, Gavin's eyes flicked around the room, never resting on anything for very long. He stood restively, weight bouncing from one foot to another. One hand was fidgeting in his jean short pocket, and he did seem like he would bolt at any second. "Would you like a coffee? Or something to eat?" At the offer of food, Gavin's wariness turned into eagerness, and he nodded.

As Mike bustled in the kitchen, it was as if a test had been passed and Gavin moved away from the door and stood in the lounge. His hands left his pocket. "I... I'm sorry... I haven't talked... to anyone for such a long time. I guess there aren't too many black Russians." He started to sob. Mike stopped what he was doing and led him to the couch. He didn't know whether he should comfort him and ended up awkwardly half patting him on the shoulder until the sobbing abated. Then he left him, extricating himself carefully because he didn't know whether Gavin was asleep or embarrassed, and completed heating him some leftover Chinese food in the microwave. He brought the bowl over with a tea towel and a fork and placed it on the table in front of Gavin, leaving again and returning with a fresh can of soft drink. Gavin stirred at the smell and wolfed down the offering, smiling his thanks though his eyes remained sad. The jolt of sugar from the soft drink brought a sigh, and Mike waited patiently. As he got close to the end of the bowl, Mike sat on the couch opposite. "So there's nothing between you and the door, you can leave anytime you want. I won't tell anyone about you, but I am very keen on learning about your story. I'm not a reporter."

Gavin watched him for a while, before putting a Swiss army knife from his pocket on the table beside the now-empty bowl. "OK. I guess I won't need this."

"Start at the beginning. What happened?"

"Ah, the beginning?" Gavin paused, arranging things in his head. "OK, about two years ago me and Gary,"—his voice caught at the mention of Gary, but he continued—"went to a cross-country race in Wales where we met a guy who was into Sat tracking."

"I'm sorry, 'Sat tracking'?"

"It's civilian satellite tracking. You get a telescope and watch the sky. You make observations and share your data. There's a network of really smart people all over the world, it's very sociable. Anyway, he suggested it would be cool if we wanted to join in. I looked it up and it struck me as something pretty cool, so I got a telescope and put it on the hotel roof. It was a neat project. I put it on a robotic stand so that the whole thing is wirelessly controllable. Auckland's light pollution isn't the best and there's a big blank spot where the Sky Tower is but apart from that I can see a lot of the sky. Most of the Sat trackers are based in the Northern Hemisphere, while the ones in the Southern Hemisphere are based in South Africa or Australia, so I was providing coverage of a sector that no one else could see."

"Oh, OK," said Mike, waiting to hear when organised crime and international banking came into it.

"So there are some satellites which race across the sky, like the International Space Station. Close to the Earth and travelling really fast. But as you get further away from the Earth you get slower and slower until, at about 36,000km, you seem from the Earth to be stationary. You're still going really fast, it's just that you're going the same speed as the point on the Earth you're above. So I'm waiting for the ISS to go past and just before it arrives in the bit of sky I'm pointing at, the sky changes."

"Huh?"

"Yeah, I know, right? So I'm looking at the sky where the ISS will go whizzing past really fast, and I've calculated exactly where that will be in the sky and I'm waiting and looking at some stars in the distance. And the stars are lightyears away, right? They've been there for aeons. The Ancient Greek and Romans wrote about these stars. Well, not these ones, these are in the Southern Hemisphere, but you know what I mean. The stars don't move except in the same way as the sky as a whole does. And I'm looking at those stars and one minute they're there and the next they are not. Not only that, but seconds later different stars—get this—totally different stars move into view. Not the same positions, but they appear out of nowhere and then slowly settle into positions."

"What do you mean different stars? Surely stars all look the same?"

Gavin didn't quite roll his eyes, but his body language indicated that Mike had said something foolish.

"So, as I said, different stars appeared and then moved into position. I rubbed my eyes because a whole bunch of Newton's laws just went flying out of the window. So I got in touch with the Sat trackers in Oz and said, you have to check out this part of the sky—some weird shit is happening."

"Why not the guys in London?" asked Mike.

"Keep up, Mike, they can't see that part of the sky—it's in the Northern

Hemisphere." Gavin saw that Mike didn't get it so picked up a decorative cane ball from a basket on the coffee table. He held it up and pointed at a spot on the bottom half. "This is us now. We can see the walls of the room, but we can't see that part of the ceiling because the Earth gets in the way. In the same way, the spot on the bottom half can see this part of the floor, but the spot on the top part of the ball can't see it because the bulge of the Earth gets in the way."

"Got it," responded Mike. "So the part of the sky where the stars moved is on the floor so you need someone who is also pointing downwards to corroborate what you saw."

"Right! So I got in touch with the Aussies. Told them where to look. They couldn't see what I was talking about. I thought they were being thick, because, you know, Aussies. But even after I told them to consult the star charts, they couldn't see it. They thought I was the slow one. They eventually sent me a picture of the star chart with a screenshot of what their telescope was telling them. Same, same. No difference. I sent them the shot I was seeing and even with the telemetry settings on the image proving that I was pointing the telescope where I said I was pointing it, they said 'Sorry, can't replicate. Check that your telescope settings are correct'."

A response seemed to be required. "Shocking!" Mike tried. Apparently, that was correct.

"Right? So I tried the South Africans. Same thing. So what that meant was that when I looked at a section of the sky, not a big section—quite tiny really—but a section of the sky, I was getting a different trio of stars than the rest of the world."

"So what did you do?" asked Mike.

"There are online tools where you can take a photo of a star and send it in and the tool will tell you which star it is and where in the sky you can see it."

"OK, and what did it say? Was it some supernova and you get to name the star after yourself?"

"No. It said it couldn't find it. And then, when I reached out to the person who ran the tool to see why, he sent back a really rude email. He said 'Yes, those stars do not exist as a part of any constellation known to man, but that if you reversed them it was obviously these three stars.' And when I looked up those three stars, they were from a totally different part of the sky! And I hadn't reversed the image before sending it to him, so I don't know what his problem was."

"So he thought you'd made some technical error with the image you'd sent him?"

Gavin indignantly nodded.

"But you hadn't. And now there's a piece of sky which is showing a mirror image of a different part of the sky, but only for you here in Auckland, not for anywhere else?"

Gavin nodded again, more thoughtfully now.

"I'm not an astronomer, but it certainly sounds like someone has put a mirror up in the sky."

"Good, it's not just me then. I sent an email to the Sat trackers to that end, laying out my findings and they were very polite but, without corroborating evidence, nobody would believe me. And here's where it got interesting," Gavin's voice lowered and Mike found himself leaning forward on the couch, drawn into the very alien story. "We were watching a very niche sport on satellite TV one night, I won't tell you what it is, and the satellite signal went out. Just like that. That was weird, we thought. It happens, but very rarely. And then I got lucky—or unlucky depending on your point of view. The next night it went out again. But this time I happened to be looking at that mysterious patch of sky through my telescope on my laptop. As soon as the signal went out I looked and the stars had disappeared and I could see a satellite looking back at me. Then after 30 minutes the stars swung back—the wrong ones—the mirrored ones, and we got reception back again."

"Was the TV show the same each night? Do you think someone was trying to stop you from seeing that show?"

Gary shook his head. "Nope, totally different show, different time as well."

"So someone can stop the satellite TV from working?"

"I guess so. I tried to figure it out. If you put a satellite into a geosynchronous orbit you could shoot a beam of energy and swamp the receiving satellite dishes who are pointing at the satellites in lower orbits with noise, effectively making the satellite useless for that part of the world."

"But who really cares if Auckland gets satellite TV? That seems like a lot of work to deprive you of your sport, however dubious it is."

"Satellite TV is only one use for satellites in those orbits, Mike. Anyway, obviously nobody else could see what I could see, so I set up my telescope to record that area of space, and waited." Gavin didn't say anything for a long time.

The penny dropped. Mike said gently, "Is that when the shooting happened?"

Gavin nodded, looking downcast and very, very weary. "And then I was out getting groceries one morning and was on my way back. I was at the end of the corridor and saw the back of a man knocking on our door. The door opened and I saw Gary who saw me behind the guy. He smiled at me. That smile. The guy asked in thickly accented English 'Gavin?', and Gary started to point at me, to say, no, but here he is. And the guy got spooked at Gary's arm coming up and started shooting wildly. I don't know where the gun came from or where he was hiding it but it wasn't loud at all. It sounded like 'thitt, thitt, thitt', really fast. Gary fell, I must have screamed, the guy turned and saw me. I ran, turned the corner and didn't want to be in a long corridor where I could get shot in the back, so I thought I'd take the lift in the service corridor. I actually thought the doors might be bulletproof, so as long as they closed before the guy got there I should be OK. But the lift was out of order so I panicked, I could hear footsteps in the hallway so I looked around and the only way out I could see was the hatch in the ceiling, so I placed one foot on the door handle and leapt up, knocking the hatch out of the way, but landing on the floor. I managed to wedge myself in the vacant hatch on the second jump and lifted myself into the ceiling gap. I swung the cover back over the hole I'd just come through and waited. And waited."

"Why didn't you call the police?"

"I was going to—I was. But then I thought about it. If the security forces in Russia were really pissed at something they thought I knew about satellites, pissed enough to try and kill me, then as soon as I emerge I'm on borrowed time. Police protection or not, it's only a matter of time before the Russians get me. You saw the efforts they took to get those spies in Britain, right?"

"You mean the Skripals with Novichok—that nerve toxin, right? And the opposition politician?"

"Opposition politician?"

"Oh, you didn't hear about that one? A Russian opposition politician had Novichok added to the seams of his underwear. He went into a coma on the plane to a political rally. The only reason he survived was that the pilot made an emergency landing and got him to a hospital. He convalesced in Germany."

"On the lining of his underwear? Oh man," Gavin shook his head. "But when it came down to it, I just didn't want... I don't want..."

"Hey, I can help you—I could call the police now, we could get them to come down and give you witness protection. I'm pretty sure that the New Zealand police force hasn't been infiltrated by the Russian mob or whoever that guy was."

The shaking became almost manic. "No! No..." then he got himself under control. "No... thank you, but no. Do you know what it's like to lose part of you? For the first week, I cried the whole time I was up there. My clothes stank and I lost a lot of weight. My phone died. I didn't care, I just cried and cried. Gary was my world. We did everything together—over 5km I had better stamina, but he was better on the short courses. He was jealous of me working freelance, not having to go into the office, but he got paid holidays, bonuses and Christmas parties. He had a way of seeing the world, of letting me know that everything would be OK. He calmed me. He said I helped him see the good in people. He was always a little cynical, a little sardonic. Anyway, I guess I was grieving. So for maybe a few days, I was a mess. I had to keep quiet too in case someone heard me. Then, eventually, and I'm not sure why, I woke up and I didn't cry. So I slipped down, and it turned out it was in the middle of the night. For some reason, I didn't want to go back into our room, and I certainly didn't want to go outside, so I ate leftover room service. I felt so ashamed. I used the staff bathrooms on the third floor. Then when they opened the gym in the morning, I used the bathrooms there. I ended up stealing a robe and some slippers because nobody bothers you if you're wandering around the hotel corridors in a robe and slippers. And that was my life. One meal a day of whatever people didn't eat. Shower and wash my clothes in the bathrooms at the gym."

"How did you get to the gym? Did you use your swipe card?"

"Yes, it still works. I have been dreading what would happen if they turned that off. I'd have to wait until someone else gets into the lift and then pat my pockets and pretend I've left my card in the room and hope they help me out. Or maybe I could steal one from the maid's cart."

"So you're pretty sure it was the Russians who were after you?"

"I know what I heard."

"And it couldn't be something that Gary was involved with at his work?"

Gavin frowned as he thought about it. "The guy at the door was asking about me by name. I'm not sure why he would have done that if Gary had been in trouble. Besides, Gary wasn't involved with clients, he managed some back office team."

"So what now? Do you climb back into the ceiling? What kind of life is that, anyway? I'm assuming you didn't go to the funeral?"

Gavin ignored the question about the funeral. "I've had a lot of time to think. The telescope on the roof has been recording since...has been recording the whole time. On an SD card."

"Wait, the telescope is still operating up there? In the cold and rain and wind?"

Gavin smiled bashfully. "Yeah, I made a housing for it which is waterproof. It's hooked into the mains power up there, so there's no reason it shouldn't have been recording data. My phone can normally adjust where it's pointing, but it's dead and I won't have data because I haven't paid my bill."

"You can charge it here if you like, I have a charger. And you can use my Wi-Fi, the password is on the router over there. Can you get the data over the phone?"

"No, I didn't know how to program that. I'm more into robotics and mechanics and that side of things. If I can get you to collect the data, I can give you an email address to send it to the other Sat trackers and they can see if there's anything there."

"Sounds easy enough, but why can't you go up there and get the SD card yourself? Sounds like it should be easy, right? Unless you're scared there's a Russian waiting up there with a gun or they've put a bomb underneath it to take you out?"

"Fuck, those windows are huge—if there's anyone in the car park they could be pointing a gun at me right now." Outside, the car park was near full, the daily commuters yet to venture out to sit in the gridlock that Auckland's motorways turned into every evening at rush hour. The clouds were slate grey and low, threatening to dump more rain, while the puddles collecting on the top level of the car park paid testament to the non-stop showers that had plagued the day.

Mike could see that Gavin was serious. "OK, how about you crouch down here below the window? That way we can still talk and you can charge your phone and nobody outside can see you. How does that sound?" Mike didn't know if Gavin was altogether mentally sound. Some of the things he'd been saying made him think he might have PTSD or be suicidal, but he was confident that he had a much better view of what was happening. "So what do you want to happen now? I can call the police for you? Or you could stay here tonight? It would be good to sleep in a proper bed, wouldn't it? You could stay the rest of this week but I'm leaving to go back to England next week. Or if you wanted help to get away, I could order an Uber and we could smuggle you out. The Russians can't cover all the exits, can they? Don't you want to see your family?"

Gavin blinked a few times. "My family disowned me when I came out. They're Jehovah's Witnesses. I told you, Gary was my life. And now he's gone." He was quiet for a while, thinking. "I don't think that the Russians know where the telescope is. We should be able to tell if it's still there when my battery charges. But yes, I think that I should probably go alone to retrieve the memory stick. It's probably not dangerous, but there's a bit of a jump between buildings to get to it which is a little disconcerting. And I'd have to describe how to get there. And there's a bit where I'm not sure someone of your size would be able to pass."

Mike laughed. "Thanks!"

Gavin got to his feet. "Thanks for the Chinese. Damn, that was good. I'll stay in my hatch tonight and if the rain holds off I'll see about getting the SD card for you. It's significantly safer getting to the telescope in the dry. And then you can send the data for me to the Sat trackers. Do you have some paper and a pen? I'll give you that address."

He played with his phone which had some battery left on it now as Mike fetched the Post-it pad and a pen from the kitchen. Gavin wrote an email address on the Post-it and then went over to the router and typed the password into his phone. A few minutes later he confirmed that the telescope was still in good working order.

"So why didn't you set it up so that you could access the data remotely as well as change where it was pointing?" asked Mike.

"I didn't think of it," responded Gavin. "I was interested in the mechanics of it, not the data." He didn't look pleased at the question, so Mike dropped it.

"So what time do you think you might go up and check it out?" asked Mike.

"The weather app says that there'll be more showers tonight and tomorrow morning, then clearing around lunchtime. I'll give the roof a couple of hours to dry out a little. The last thing I want is to slip up there and take a tumble. It's a seven-storey drop if I get it wrong. I'll come past, maybe 2:30pm or 3pm with the SD card."

'I'll have lunch ready for you," said Mike, seeing Gavin to the door.

THE RESEARCH

Mike sat down on the couch, deep in thought. First of all, he needed to see if he had any legal exposure. The police were probably looking for Gavin, but that didn't put any onus on Mike to tell them that he'd spoken to Gavin. Would the police consider Gavin a suspect? Mike couldn't see how: New Zealand was like the UK in terms of gun control laws, so if Gavin or Gary had a gun it would be registered. And unlikely to match the details of that which was used to kill Gary. If Gavin had killed Gary, why do it at the doorstep of their apartment. And why from the outside? No, the police wouldn't consider Gavin a suspect, so Mike wouldn't be guilty of harbouring a suspect, or aiding and abetting, or whatever the local version of that crime might be. The SD card with the data on it wasn't evidence of any crime, unless it was the Russians and they were doing something dodgy up in space. Surely that wouldn't be in the local cops' jurisdiction though. Mike had made some promises to Gavin in the heat of the moment which he realised he would have to make good on. For one thing, he'd promised not to tell anyone that Gavin was here.

He looked at his watch. It was a little after 3:30pm—about 24 hours before the SD card would show up. And about 4:40am in the Northern Hemisphere. If the email address in question was manned by someone there then it would be at least a few hours before they would be able to communicate with him. He should have asked Gavin if he could tell the Sat trackers about him. That would explain why he was sending them a whole bunch of data to analyse.

He'd love to be able to crunch that data himself, but he knew he didn't have any of the domain knowledge necessary to know what to do, and to which parts of the data. While he knew a bunch of geometrical functions from some work he'd done with Google Maps and property data, he knew enough to know that celestial geometry would be in three dimensions and would need a lot more maths that he didn't have. Best to leave the experts to do the crunching.

But what he could do while waiting for the Sat trackers to wake up was do some research himself. The Sat trackers' website was surprisingly light on real data, their blog sparsely populated with entries and most of them commenting on articles they'd linked to from other sites.

Disappointed, Mike cast his net wider.

Hours ticked by. He'd started with basic Google searches—definition type searches, giving as starting points LEO, MEO and GEO. He disappeared down a rabbit hole following what high earth orbit meant—for when there are low and medium somethings, surely there would be high somethings too?

He branched out after that to see how many satellites were in each zone. It turned out there were a lot, with maybe a quarter actually operational, the remainder being old ones, described in one article as "space debris".

Another rabbit hole filled at least an hour of his time with discussions of satellite killers, missiles and Cold War era plans for laser weapons to bring down satellites. It seemed that the desire to rob the enemy of satellite resources had been around for a very long time.

Mike was proud of his investigative skills when he found one website describing a US launch being delayed and then changed at short notice to fly near the International Space Station. The dates lined up very nicely for reports of the Russians not divulging the contents of an experiment being sent up to the ISS. They were obviously going up to have a closer look at something parked at the ISS.

He was a little disappointed that the anti-Satellite weapons seemed to be limited to flying a satellite close to the target and detonating a bomb on board like some sort of cosmo-suicide-bomber. It seemed like a waste. And a one-use weapon as well. There was mention of more sophisticated satellites though—ones that could sneak up on their target and either plant a small explosive on them or else just snip the wires from their solar array to disconnect them from a power source. He snorted to himself when he saw the accompanying image: a giant pair of scissors flying through space like some cartoon.

He'd just finished a few posts on historical anti-satellite usages, when he noticed that he was getting hungry. Just before he started cooking his dinner, he decided to send the Sat trackers an email to let them know that the satellite data was on its way and if they could crunch the data and let him know what they found. It would be, what, 7am their time? Maybe they'd get back to him before bed, maybe not. Either way, it would be off his plate.

He didn't feel like anything extravagant so elected to cook a stir fry. The supermarket nearby had ready-made meal ingredients so all he really had to do was fry the cubes of pork and then add the vegetables and sauce. His contribution to the recipe was to add a handful of cashews. Hardly cordon-bleu cooking!

He finished dinner, cleaned up and spent some more time researching satellites when he decided to get an early night. He still hadn't heard back from the Sat trackers, so thought he'd ait and wake to some sort of reply rather than sitting on tenterhooks on the off chance that one came through. He was just turning out the lights in the lounge when his phone rang.

"Jim here. Hey, I'm doing security down here and on my break I had a cigarette with our friends from the hotel, and I asked them about the utility room. Apparently, the only thing in there is the endpoint for the fibre optics with the internet connections. All the real utilities are handled differently.

The electricity is managed centrally and so goes into the basement, while the water and gas are in the plant room around the back."

"Ah awesome, thanks for that. Good work."

'So are you going to tell me what all this is about?"

"Uh... I can't just yet. I'll tell you as soon as I can, I promise. But thanks for that, I do owe you one."

Mike was a bit distracted by everything he'd learnt during the day and so headed to bed, wondering what kind of response he'd get to his email.

He woke leisurely at about 8am, stretched and checked his emails. Sure enough, there was a reply from the Sat trackers. He'd had to be vague with the wording of his message, not wanting to refer to Gavin by name or to the nature of the telescope data that he would be sending. As a result, the response was very lukewarm—tepid even. They did not see the point in sending telescope data. He was just trying to word a response to their response that would somehow communicate the origin of the data, plus the circumstances around its acquisition, when he stopped dead in his tracks.

Why was he trying to get the wording right?

With financial crime, as he well knew from experience at work, one of the worst things you could do was to tip off the suspect in an investigation. If they were clever enough to cover their tracks, you normally needed to catch them in the act. If they got wind of an investigation then they would change their behaviour and, even if they put their offending on ice for three months, if those were the three months that you were getting paid to do the investigation, you would end up with suspicions but no proof. No proof meant no conviction and no conviction meant that it would be a customer review of "We spent a lot of money and we ended up with the same suspicions that we started with" instead of "Great job, bad guy in jail, money well spent".

So he found himself writing to the Sat trackers in the same nebulous, cards-close-to-the-chest manner that he had employed at work. In case he tipped someone off. But the only people he could be in danger of tipping off were the Russians. And the only way that they could intercept the email traffic was if they compromised his laptop. Or the Sat trackers computer. Or somehow intercepted the traffic between the two by employing a Man in the Middle attack. But in order to do that they would need to have physical access to the network connections between the laptop and the router in Mike's room. Or he thought, as his stomach dropped, if they had access to the connection to the hotel room he was standing in and the outside world. The connection would go through the utility room. The utility room which had been broken into.

He recalled the first time he'd had to explain a Man in the Middle attack to some of the juniors on an engagement. He'd got a router, set it up in his hotel room, in such a way to log all the traffic through it, then set the name of it to "hotel name_ Guest" and no password. His room had been on the first floor, not too far from the hotel restaurant, so they'd been in range when they had dinner. He got the junior colleagues to log on to the guest Wi-Fi and make a search. After that, he logged on to the router remotely and showed them the log of their activities. He followed up the lesson by explaining that if any step in the hops that the traffic took from device to server were compromised then the messages would be intercepted. Ginny was one of the juniors and had thought for a second before asking about encryption—if the message was encrypted, wouldn't that just give the interceptors the garbled, encrypted message? Mike had to agree that was the case but added that anyone going to the trouble of intercepting the traffic may have the resources to decrypt the message.

Mike thought about all the research he'd done the night before. All the websites about satellites and anti-satellite weapons. His email stating that he had a whole bunch of satellite data to be processed. He might as well have painted a giant bullseye on his back. These people had gunned down a man on his doorstep to try and prevent analysis of exactly that sort of data. All of a sudden it seemed that subtlety and nuance in an email didn't really belong. Mike wasn't smiling now.

He drafted a new email, laying out the data he was expecting from Gavin, saying that it was imperative that they analyse it to see if they could identify the satellite. As he typed, Mike suddenly came to the conclusion that he couldn't send the data via email. It would show the Russians everything that they knew. Now that he had inadvertently shown the Russians who would be receiving the data, they were in danger. And presumably their internet connections would soon be compromised in the same or similar way to how his own had been. So he couldn't even share the files on a cloud storage site and send them a link—that too would be intercepted.

Dammit! He'd screwed things up. He'd been in holiday mode and—no, he decided, I won't blame myself, that won't help anyone. If the Russians hadn't murdered anyone else in the Sat trackers, then maybe they were focused purely on Gavin. All he had to do was make sure they received the data in person. Impossible to intercept that with a Man in the Middle attack.

He changed the email. He said that as a result of potential communication security compromise, he would have to hand-deliver the data. And that he would be in touch shortly to arrange a time to hand the data over. Then he got the pad of Post-it notes and changed the settings on his phone to ignore the Wi-Fi connection. He checked the text message from his cell phone service provider, the one he'd received when he had landed in Auckland telling him how much data would cost while he was in New Zealand. Sighing at the exorbitant cost, he brought up a browser and searched for the phone numbers of the two airlines for the return trip to England.

An hour of listening to on-hold music later, he finally found out what it would cost him to move his tickets forward. He was extremely fortunate that there was availability—so he'd be able to leave at 7pm that same night and only spend an hour in Sydney, before the long hop across to London with a brief stop in the Middle East. And it only cost £500 for the privilege.

He'd remembered what Gavin had said the day before about the car park being the perfect spot for a sniper, so he left the curtains pulled. The weather outside was grey but the puddles were smaller and he hoped Gavin didn't have any issues on the roof.

He packed his bag, taking his time, and double and triple checked the bathroom and closet because he was so distracted. He was thinking about three things at once—the immediate task of packing; what would happen at each of the airports; and then what would happen at the end of his flight. The overarching umbrella of uncertainty derailed the application of any real logical thinking about his situation. He'd been on some engagements which had a certain element of danger—going to an African nation for their governmental budget and expenditure information; extracting data in an Eastern European office block in the middle of the night; and investigating a Swiss bank's vaults being the top three. But he'd been in control of the situation a lot more on each of those occasions. Now he didn't know if the Russians had monitored his web traffic, had the logs but hadn't looked at them yet, or were on their way to the room with some sort of death squad. He didn't know whether he would be safer in the room, in the lobby, in a different hotel or getting a head start to the airport. All he knew was that he needed to be in his room when Gavin returned with the SD card and, if Gavin didn't show up, he'd have to try and clamber onto the roof to find the telescope.

He calmed himself and took a seat on the couch. Think about what you can control, he thought to himself. I need to say goodbye to Jim. I need to get the SD card from Gavin. I need to leave the country. I need to get the SD card to the Sat track people. Oh! I need to find out what the contact at Sat track looks like. He'd seen too many movies where the bad guys kill the good guy and take their place to intercept things. I need to make some sort of backup of the data, but not on the Wi-Fi connecting from the hotel room.

He was fortunate that checking out of the room did not require interacting with the hotel staff—the management of the room was independent of the hotel. All he had to do was pull the door closed behind himself with the swipe cards inside, then the cleaner who was booked for the end of the stay would collect them and pass them on to the management company for the next guest.

Mike suddenly remembered that he'd promised Gavin some food and dashed across to the kitchenette to see what was in the fridge. He looked at his watch. It was a little after 1pm. So if he went out and got some food, he could be back in time for Gavin to drop off the SD card, drop into the pub to say goodbye to Jim and then grab a taxi to the airport. Then he would go to an airport lounge while he waited for his flight. It was only a short transit in Sydney which probably meant it wasn't worth seeking out the lounge there, a similarly small stop off in Doha, and then arriving in London at midday local time. If he could find out the contact details for the person in the UK, he could either hire a car or go straight there and give them the SD card. Call it six hours in New Zealand waiting for the flight, 30 hours in the air or airports and then maybe four hours at the other end depending on where this person was. Hopefully, he'd be able to get some sleep on the plane. But before all that: food. And if a hit squad were coming for him at his apartment, if he happened to be out getting food, then they wouldn't find him there. As he grabbed his keys and wallet and slipped on his blazer, he realised that if the hit squad couldn't get into the hotel, then they might be waiting for him in the lobby. That thought made the journey down the lift a bit nerve-wracking—he was going to have to get better at controlling the meanderings of his mind!

He strolled, with a totally false nonchalance, through the lobby from the lifts to the front door and headed out into the still chilly air towards the supermarket in the middle of town. What a marvellous location for a hotel—close enough to the casino, a short stroll to the supermarket and a short walk from the bus and train terminals. He realised he was distracting himself with pablum to mask the panic that was barely kept in check. He stepped past a man begging outside the supermarket and headed towards the ready-to-eat section near the entrance. If he hadn't eaten anything except leftover room service, what would he be looking for? Fresh fruit maybe? A salad? He ended up getting a couple of salads, a turkey and salad roll, a couple of packets of crisps and a pair of soft drinks, all in a plastic bag.

As he got closer to the hotel on his return, his pace slowed until, by the time he reached the lobby, he really wasn't at all keen on heading up to his room. He decided to kill some time in the lobby and have his salad there instead. The staff at the coffee kiosk in the lobby were only too happy to provide him with a little fork for eating his salad. He kept a close eye on the door, giving a jump whenever anyone came in. It was close to 2pm when he pulled himself together and finally headed up.

Once he got to his room door, he let out a deep breath and tapped the swipe card to the reader and pushed his way inside. The room was as he'd left it and a quick scamper through it looking behind doors and inside wardrobes revealed a distinct lack of hitmen. He got his packed bag ready on the floor by the door, the bag with the food in it on the bench beside the door. He grabbed a fork from the drawer and put it in the bag with the food, then tried to relax on the couch.

The knock at the door almost gave him a heart attack. He looked through the peephole before unlocking.

It was Gavin. Mike ushered him into the apartment. The first thing Gavin noticed was the packed bag, and he looked at Mike with a frown. Mike gave him the food bag and then tried to explain.

"Did you know there had been a break-in at the hotel after the... shooting?"

Gavin shook his head.

"The Utility Room was broken into."

"OK..." Gavin said, not getting it.

"The Utility Room is where the internet comes into and leaves the building. They didn't take anything, but I suspect that the Russians are eavesdropping on the internet traffic for the entire hotel."

"I still don't get it. Why's that important?"

"After our conversation yesterday I wanted to know more about the things you'd brought up."

"OK"

"So there'll be a sizable spike in internet traffic with search terms like 'satellites', 'orbits', 'killer satellites' and that sort of thing. A bit of an obvious clue for anyone monitoring the traffic coming out of the hotel. And even if they don't know that you're alive, they know someone in this particular flat was very, very interested in the subject."

"Oh, shit."

"Yeah, so it might not be such a good idea using the flat internet connection. Or to stay here. I'm getting on the next plane out of the country and will hand-deliver the SD card. Tell me what Heath Cox looks like. The last thing I want to do is hand the data over to the wrong person."

"Uh, so Heath is about my height, slim as well, but he's got a great beard, not long, but very thick - he keeps it short, neat and trim."

"Is he on social media? Is it easy to find a photo of him?"

Gavin frowned, thinking. "I guess you might find a photo at a conference or something. Maybe one of the cross-country meets a few years back."

"OK, so maybe not something easy to get. Look, that's fine. I promised you some lunch, so there's a bunch of food in the bag. I'm going to head to the airport. I don't want to hang around here at all. I'd advise telling your story to the local police though—it's the only way to get things back to normal. And you do want to go back to normal... don't you?"

Gavin handed over the SD card slowly. He seemed miles away. "Things will never be back to normal. But do me a favour. Make sure Gary didn't die in vain, OK?"

Mike placed the SD card in his inside pocket and tapped it from the outside to see what it felt like nestled in the pocket with his passport and wallet. "I'll try," he said as he placed the room card keys on the bench in the kitchen and picked up his bag. Gavin picked up the food bag and headed out the door. Mike followed him and then turned to watch the door close. When he turned back to say goodbye to Gavin, he had already gone.

Jim was surprised to see him so early in the day, doubly so when he saw the wheelie bag. "I just came down to say goodbye and thanks for the hospitality, Jim. I've got to head back to the UK at short notice, but you've made the holiday one to remember. If you find yourself over my half of the world, let me know and I'll return the favour."

"Oh definitely, thanks for that. Yeah, it's been real, man. I assume you'll tell me what's going on when you can, I thought you had another week to go? It must be pretty important to miss out on a week of holiday, huh?"

Mike thought about what was driving his behaviour. He could just go to the police with the whole story. But he'd promised Gavin that he wouldn't. And the reasons he was giving the Sat trackers the data was because he'd told Gavin that he would and because he hoped that would mean whatever bullseye was painted on his back would disappear. With the likelihood that he was being pursued by killers, he thought it best to move quickly to unburden himself of the data.

"Yes, definitely important. I've got your phone number, so I'll get in touch when I can tell you more."

"OK, bro. Take care of yourself. And don't do anything I wouldn't do."

"Will do, Jim, will do."

THE RETURN

Auckland Airport was like every other airport Mike had been to over his many years living out of a suitcase for work. Check-in desks, security checkpoint, shops, gates and lounges. And endless open corridors and queues between them. The only benefits of smaller airports over the multi-terminal monstrosities of the continent were the shorter distances to the gates. But first he had to check-in.

He handed over his passport and set his wheeled suitcase on the machine to be weighed, happy that he'd travelled light so that, even with the 2kg disagreement between the kitchen scales and the official weighing machine, he was still well under his weight allowance. As he waited for all the boarding passes to be printed, he asked how full the flights were. The lady behind the desk was very helpful, barely pausing before indicating that the Auckland to Sydney was about half full, the Sydney to Doha about a quarter full and the Doha to London totally full. She handed back his passport with the three boarding passes and luggage receipt before announcing that his luggage would be waiting for him in London on his arrival—it had been checked all the way through. She mentioned that the lounge was through security, through duty-free and to the right. He thanked her and headed towards security.

Mike thought he could tell the time of the year by the demographic of his fellow passengers. No hordes of students, so it wasn't the beginning or end of term time. Mind you that was more prevalent in the UK—the proximity to the continent made ski and culture holidays more practical.

The lack of family groups meant that it wasn't a significant holiday like Thanksgiving, Easter or Christmas. Mike wasn't sure if the lack of passenger numbers was due to the smaller airport size or it being mid-winter, but the number of suited men carrying briefcases certainly indicated it was a Thursday or Friday. Many of the consulting and accounting firms would send you to the client site for Monday to Thursday, bringing you back to your "home office" for the Friday.

Mike had "priority" stamped on his boarding pass, so went to the special queue for the business class traveller. There the line had only one other person, a suited and booted Australian who got through the security check with the minimum of fuss. Mike got through quickly too, the only noteworthy episode being when the family of four following him into the queue were turned away due to not having priority status. Back they went to the regular queues.

Mike had relaxed since arriving at the airport. He was on his turf now, he thought. The downside of travelling for work was that you frequently only saw the insides of taxis, hotels, offices and airports. An acquaintance had compared travel histories and gasped in wonder at the number of places that had appeared on Mike's list, but was less astonished when Mike had told him that most of those countries he had not actually seen, just visited for work and hadn't really explored. Less than a sixth of his trips had been for fun—far fewer, in both number and total duration than the acquaintance had achieved. As mitigation for losing the passport measuring contest, Mike retorted that at least he had the points. Ah yes, the mountain of hotel and airline loyalty points accumulated over the years would come in handy when he could properly travel for fun!

He headed to the lounge, showing his boarding pass and passport. He parked his bag on a chair beside the window and headed back the way he'd come for some food. They had small buns loaded with camembert, salami and caramelised onions, so he loaded his plate with three, paused to add a can of ginger ale from the nearby fridge and returned to his seat. His window had a pretty uninspiring view, looking out over the roof of the rest of the airport terminal. In the far distance he could just make out the top of the tail of a plane, but that was all the clues that he was at an airport. He could have been in a shopping mall or even a warehouse somewhere. At least there was natural light, even if the clouds were conspiring to hide the sunset in the distance.

He looked at his watch. Boarding wouldn't be for another couple of hours, so he got out his laptop and turned it on. He ran his antivirus software and when that had finished, got out the SD card. He was fortunate that his laptop had an SD card reader built-in. He ran his antivirus software on the SD card too. Then he checked out the size of the files. In total they came to 40GB, too big for him to send as an attachment in an email but small enough for him to upload to his cloud storage. He connected to the lounge internet and uploaded the files, making sure to grab a link to the whole folder. He went into his emails and copied the email address of one of his closest friends, Tim. Then he went into the folder on the cloud storage and added Tim to the permissions. Finally, he wrote an email to Tim. Short and sweet. "If I don't talk to you by Monday, could you please get these files to this email address?" And then he included the Sat tracker email that Gavin had given him. Just in case, he added the Sat tracker email address to the folder directly. Now, as long as the Sat trackers had the link to the cloud storage, they should be able to get the files, regardless of what happened to the physical SD card. He disconnected the SD card and placed it back in his inside jacket pocket beside his wallet.

He still did not want to just send the link to the Sat trackers. If the Russians had indeed compromised the Sat trackers computers, then he would be confirming that they had the data and put their lives at risk. And Tim? While Mike definitely felt bad about potentially putting him in danger, Mike needed some safety net, just in case he met a sticky end on the way back home to the UK. Mike breathed out heavily. He could never be a spy, he decided. The uncertainty! The double and triple backup plans. But mainly the paranoia. Ah well, he was OK now. Not quite the ending he was looking for from his holiday.

The files taken care of, he had nothing to do until his flight boarded, so settled in and watched some topical comedy shows on YouTube. It was the least boring way of catching up on the news—watching comedians mock it.

When his flight was called, he made his way the short distance to the gate. He kept alert but didn't know quite what he was looking for. That didn't stop him from examining every face with ears pricked for anything vaguely Slavic sounding. All in vain though.

While the Auckland to Sydney flight had been comfortable enough on a Boeing 737-800, with the seats reminiscent of a Lazy Boy in deep brown leather laid out in a 2-2 formation, the other two legs of the flight would be on a widebody long-haul jet with lie-flat seats, and Mike was looking forward to seeing if he could get some sleep. After landing, the business class passengers were let off first and Mike made his way towards the nearest departures board to see which gate his flight to Doha was leaving from. It turned out that it wasn't far at all, the gate was only just beyond where the lounge was. Mike headed over and found a seat with the rest of the people waiting around gate 53.

He frowned a little. It seemed that the lady behind the counter at Auckland might have just been referring to the numbers of business class passengers when she said it was a quarter full. It looked like there were a couple of hundred people waiting to board.

After about twenty an announcement asked for anyone needing additional help or had children with them to come forward. A straggly line formed of young families, Mike smirking as one of the munchkins chose that time to go for a run, pursued by their harried parents. The gate staff made short work of the queue and sent the stream of parents and children down the ramp beyond. They called for business passengers next and Mike made his way to the front of the queue. A slight delay at the entrance to the plane caused a backlog up the corridor causing Mike to queue behind the families. The child being carried by her mother in front of him gazed steadily at him, clutching a stuffed animal. Mike grinned back, but the little girl just stared. As they moved forward a few paces Mike could see that the corridor split with a sign indicating that the business passengers should take the left-hand side to their own front door to the plane. The families had expanded to completely fill the corridor though, so short of pushing his way through, Mike had to wait in line until he came to the split in the corridor naturally. He was happy enough, shuffling step by step as the queue inched its way forward. As they shuffled forward another couple of steps the staring child decided to drop their stuffed animal. Mike bent to pick it up just as the mother noticed that her load had lightened by the weight of one stuffed lamb. By that time they'd reached the split in the corridor so he was able to tuck the lamb between mother and child and head to the front door.

The airline was Qatar's second international airline who had taken great care to copy the national carrier in as many facets of the flight experience from their more famous countrymen. This included the wholesale rip-off of the cabin design based on the Qsuites, differentiated solely by changing the interior colours.

A pair of flight attendants waited at the front door and welcomed him aboard. Upon seeing his boarding pass, the head attendant nodded and asked him if he could follow her. She led him to 3F instead of 5A, the seat on his boarding pass. He frowned and she said that in order to balance out the load the pilot needed him to sit in 3F instead and that she hoped that was alright.

He smiled and said of course that was fine and settled into the seat, placing his day pack holding his laptop in the overhead bin. Mike had travelled in economy where things like that happened, especially with sparsely populated flights. It was a legitimate exercise and normally would not have caused any concern at all. However, given the events of the past few days, alarm bells were ringing loudly in Mike's head.

As he got himself squared away, he swapped his bottle of water with the one in the seat beside his. The cabin layout was an unusual seating arrangement. Basically, it was 1-2-1 (one seat by the window, an aisle, two seats in the middle, an aisle and then the other single window seat), but the odd-numbered rows were facing backwards. He'd heard that the last seats to get assigned were the central two because by then the airline would know if they had a group of four passengers travelling together. There were special options for the middle bank of seats—they could make the seats up into a double bed for any of the middle two seats facing the same way. The entertainment screen wasn't directly in front of the passenger in these seats, instead being slightly off to one side. The partition separating the pair of seats from those facing them in the row in front could be lowered, allowing a group of four to converse, play cards or eat together. He was supposed to have one of the 1- of the 1-2-1 layout - a single seat facing the rear of the plane in the back of the front of the two business class sections, and now found himself in the middle of the cabin, still facing the rear, but now with the potential for a travelling companion.

Cathy came and introduced herself. She was tall and thin and elegant, a wisp of lace attached to her hat satisfying the cultural requirement for head covering. She'd be his personal attendant for the trip and if he needed anything, anything at all, he had just to ask. They had a menu for him to peruse and select what he would like to eat, and would he like a drink or some nuts to start with?

Mike looked around. A few other passengers were in the business class section and while there weren't many of them, they still outnumbered the attendants, so he was taking "personal" with a grain of salt. He was a little concerned about the shift in seats so declined a drink or snack and instead settled down and waited. Someone was manoeuvring him. If it was the

Russians, he was worried about poisoning—that did seem the assassination technique of the day. His mind rotated through a decade of news headlines—polonium ingested in a cup of tea (how very Cold War!), Novichok smeared on a door handle or in someone's underwear. All of a sudden the smoked salmon tartare with mushrooms and dill prawns followed by the grilled beef tenderloin sounded a lot more dangerous than airline food justified.

When she arrived, he wasn't surprised. In fact, he was pleased that they had chosen such an obvious person. She was gorgeous. He'd seen photos of models, of wives and girlfriends of football players, of Instagrammers—definitely in that company. She must have been in her late twenties, with elfin features and blonde hair arranged in a complicated plait. She smiled down at him and asked if the seat beside him was 3E? He nodded. She took off her jacket and placed it on the jacket holder on the edge of the seat. Mike gulped involuntarily. She was wearing a sheer blouse which allowed a tantalising glimpse of a lace bra. Mike looked away and calculated the hours remaining before they landed in Doha. Sixteen hours. Your challenge, Mike, he told himself with eyes closed, is to rebuff, refuse and reject any and all overtures of physical contact or food from the most gorgeous physical specimen of womanhood he'd ever seen and, let's face it, that he was ever likely to see, for a period of sixteen hours. All while he hadn't had any, er, interactions for well over a year.

She settled into the seat beside him and chose from the selection of champagnes on the menu. When the attendant came over she elegantly asked for a glass of the Lallier Grand Reserve. It arrived very shortly thereafter, accompanied with a little dish of heated almonds. She sipped the champagne and grimaced, noting Mike watching her wrinkle her nose. "... And it's the best they had, not a lot of selection really, don't you think?"

Mike thought about the two pages in the menu devoted to champagnes and nodded as if it was self-evident that there was not a single acceptable vintage among the twenty on offer. "Terrible. Which airline has better though?" he asked to keep her talking.

She paused to think about it, crossing her legs and inclining her body towards his. "I had a glass of the 2002 Dom Perignon on a Singapore Airlines flight recently which was nice. And it's always lovely when they serve a Krug Grand Cuvee."

"What vintage of the Krug do you prefer?" he asked.

She was momentarily silent, surprised by the question. An instant later she broke into an exaggerated chortle. "Oh, you are a hoot. You know very well that the Krug is a blend. I'm Lana," she said holding her hand out.

He pretended not to see her hand and bowed his head in her direction. "Charmed," he said as he raised his head to meet her eyes. "I'm Mike."

She took another tiny sip, the picture of friendliness. "Well, Mike, I think we're going to be neighbours for the next sixteen hours. Tell me your life story! It's the best way of filling the hours. Better than terrible movies and TV programs, don't you agree? Far more... intimate."

She reminded him in a way of some of the partners at the consulting firms that he'd worked with—people who'd spent decades enjoying the finest food and wine (always billed to the client) and who needed to share the benefit of their opinions of which £240 bottle of wine tasted better than the other. It wasn't only the rich though, he had equally opinionated friends with strong opinions on the relative strengths of one microbrewery ale over another. It seemed everybody wanted to be the expert on something, even if it was just down to taste.

"And yourself, Lana? What brings you to Doha?"

She laughed, showing a mouth of perfect teeth. "Oh, I'm just doing some modelling there. Stand around for a few hours in hair and make-up, a few more hours, click, click, then back on the plane and head back home."

"Oh, you're based in Sydney?"

She stretched like a cat, the picture of self-satisfaction. "I'm a citizen of the world. My work takes me all over the place but yes, home happens to be in Sydney at the moment."

In the background, the in-flight briefing showed on the personal entertainment systems as the plane taxied out to the runway. The volume of the briefing was low enough for them to easily ignore it as they continued their conversation. Not long afterwards they accelerated down the runway and angled into the air.

"Where are you from originally?"

"It's a tiny village on the outskirts of Murmansk. You've probably never heard of it."

"Murmansk? In Russia?"

Lana looked surprised. "Yes, in Russia."

"My geography is pretty good—Murmansk is up near the Arctic circle, right? Santa Claus country. Funny, you don't sound Russian."

"I went to school in England, which explains the slight accent, I suppose. Lana is actually short for Svetlana. I don't usually tell people that I'm Russian." She leaned in, the picture of someone about to confide a deep secret. "People think that Russians are baddies. You see it all the time in movies and terrible books. Some balding muscle man with tattoos and a thick Russian accent doing unspeakable things." She cocked her head and smiled coquettishly. "Do I look like a baddie to you Mike?"

Mike smiled back. "Well, you have to admit that... certain Russians have not exactly been the goodies."

Lana pouted, looking very cute. "But we're not all like that, are we? So why do they make us the baddies?"

Mike looked thoughtful, stroking his chin. "I guess it's plugging into the Cold War mentality of hating the enemy. And then when the Wall came down and the War was over, the enemy du jour was based in the Middle East. But if you make the baddies generically Middle Eastern, that's a bit racist."

In a thick faux Russian accent, Lana replied. "And if the baddies all talk like this, isn't that just as racist?"

"Probably as much as making people that look like me into car thieves and drug dealers, right? But what's the alternative? If you make the hero a Russian, you have to make the movie twice as long to explain why the audience should shrug off all the media references they've learned that Russian equals baddie. Their backstory becomes the story. And all the time the audience has to fight what they've been told in every other movie and TV program. Easier to paint in primary colours so the audience understands and can accept without thinking."

"That's terrible," Lana said, holding her hand to her chest, "I'm destined to always be the baddie."

"Oh you poor dear," Mike said with a disbelieving grin, "however will you cope? Eventually, a groundswell of local Russian artists will create some magnificent movie that will paint their countrymen in the correct light and that will erase the years of bias, stigma and prejudice. And then we can all dance together down the street to equality."

"You're mocking me."

Mike paused. "Try being black in a white-collar office."

"Surely there must be some benefits? Some additional attention? Some curiosity as to what they say about black men?"

Mike let that line sit there for a while. After enough of a pause, he looked over in her direction. "About as much curiosity as there is in the roles available to a beautiful woman in the Russian mob."

She looked shocked and was silent for a while. He wondered if he'd gone too far. She continued as if he hadn't said anything, but her playful innuendo seemed a little hollow. "So no workplace relationships then? No innocent young intern?"

He shook his head. "No way, too much of a power imbalance. I prefer my partners to be my equals."

She giggled. "No, really? You don't want to teach the eager young intern what Mike likes in the bedroom?"

"I prefer it to be a mutual lesson, learning what they like too. If they're just starting out in their career, they don't usually know what they like in the bedroom. And if it's all about me, I'm not getting any pleasure from being a contributing partner in the relationship."

Lana had a faraway look on her face—the only time Mike hadn't seen her fixated on him. After only a second, she refocused on him. "I know what you mean. I think that people would be a lot happier if they realised that sexual compatibility was the number one indicator of whether a relationship will last."

"What do you mean?"

"When you ask your friends why they broke up in a relationship, they always have some excuse: we were on different pages, he wasn't mature enough, she was a psycho. But what they're really saying is 'they didn't do that thing I like with their tongue'. Because if you're happy in the bedroom, like really, really happy, then nothing else matters."

Mike shook his head emphatically. "I don't know that I believe that at all," he managed, thinking of Rachel in Auckland amongst others. "Sometimes it's just bad timing."

She looked at him over the top of her wine glass, analysing him. "Or maybe you've never been truly happy in the bedroom...? I had one client who couldn't walk after one of my visits..."

Mike blinked. Client? Was that a slip? "So what's really happening here, Svetlana? Who's paying you to spend time with me?"

She continued to eye him over her drink before answering.

"I do hospitality work for... a Russian guy. Sometimes in Europe, sometimes in Australia, sometimes in the Middle East. All over. A great job to see the world. Drink with the bigwigs, laugh at their jobs, that sort of thing. They mentioned that you were travelling from Sydney and that I should get to know you. Make sure you enjoy your flight."

Mike let out a deep breath and felt some tension leave his shoulders that he didn't know that he was carrying. So she wasn't trying to kill him after all. Then the paranoia kicked back in: how many assassins told their victims that they were going to kill them? "That's very nice of them. You'll have to give me their number so that I can thank them personally."

Svetlana smiled back. "I'm more used to people asking for my phone number, Mike."

Mike nodded. "I'm sure you do, Lana." He'd inadvertently sounded a little cold in his response, thinking about the possibility of her being an assassin. She sensed him emotionally receding and so turned to face him.

"Oh, yes. It's a danger of the job. One guy I hung out with became quite taken with me." A "cat that got the cream" smile flitted across her face. "He sent me all sorts of messages. Do you want to see?"

Mike saw an opportunity. He smiled and got his phone out too. "Definitely. It has happened to me too, let me show you." As he got out his phone he bumped the flight attendant call button. He reached over and looked at her phone. There was a text message conversation on the screen, full of plaintive pleading and declarations of unending love. His timing was impeccable. As the flight attendant asked if there was anything she could get him, he saw Lana's eyes flick up to the attendant. At that point, he took a photo of the conversation on Lana's phone with his own phone while she was looking at the attendant. While he put away his phone he turned to the attendant and asked for a ginger ale. He turned back to Lana and said "Wow, that was intense."

She smiled and pulled closer to him, angling her phone so that they both could read it at the same time which put her very close to him. She smelled great. She swiped to a different conversation, where the guy in question was promising her the world, promising to leave his wife for her, that sort of thing. "A little sad, no?" she whispered. "Fun is fun. He couldn't see that our time was limited."

"What did he do when you explained that?"

Something flickered behind her eyes and she changed the subject.

"And, of course, if there are more entertainers than entertainees, you end up with all sorts of odd combinations. Arms and legs everywhere."

He liked the sound of that but she was getting a little too close and he was enjoying her presence a little bit too much. "Tell me about your... Russian agent," he suggested, as he accepted the ginger ale from the flight attendant.

She leant back and watched him carefully. "Tell me Mike... are you married? Girlfriend?" He shook his head. "Well, you're not gay, and not a virgin. Do you have a strong relationship with God?"

The penny dropped. She wanted to know why he wasn't into her. He shook his head, while she continued.

"It's just that someone has spent a lot of money arranging things so that we can spend some time together, but I think that if you had your way then you'd prefer it if they hadn't. I'm just curious as to why that is? What should I tell Dimitri? Shall I say that Mike preferred redheads?" Even when she was probing delicate subjects she managed to make the tone playful, teasing... seductive.

Mike thought back to what Rachel had said on their last date. About how sometimes it was better to forego the night of passion to keep yourself ready for the relationship when it does come along. It was bullshit then and it was bullshit now, but he still didn't want to have Novichok rubbed on his nuts.

"Well, I would hate to think someone did not get value for their money, of course. But I can't help wondering who my mysterious benefactor is. I don't like owing people for things I haven't ordered, as much as I might enjoy them. It's like sending back an expensive gift with a 'Oh no, this is too much, I couldn't possibly'. I also don't want to insult anyone. Is there someone I could talk to and explain myself?"

Lana smiled, but it was a cold smile that didn't touch her eyes. "I don't think that's a very good idea," she said. Gone was the flirtation, gone was the spotlight that had been shone on him. While he had been a little scared and very worried about it when it was on, he didn't realise how much he'd been warmed by it. He shrugged and hit the call button. A breath later Cathy appeared, enquiring if he'd like something to eat?

"I think Svetlana and I would prefer separate seats if possible. Are there any seats with windows vacant?"

Cathy looked from one to the other uncertainly. After Svetlana gave her the smallest of small nods, she agreed that there was possibly a seat available and took Mike to his originally ticketed seat. Cathy got him squared away and when she was going past him to see to Svetlana he very quietly told her that he'd tell everyone that he spent the whole time with Svetlana so that she got her money. She looked like she'd been slapped and hurried away.

Mike closed the sliding door which separated the seat from the aisle and checked that the SD card was still in his inside pocket of his jacket. The familiar lump was there so he sighed in relief. There were still way too many hours ahead of him but he was less worried about getting killed than he had been at the beginning of the flight. He could still be wrong and if he went to sleep Svetlana might lean over the walls of his Suite and plunge a syringe into his neck—but he was hopeful that it wouldn't happen. Smiling to himself, he navigated the touchscreen and started to find movies and TV programs to fill the hours to Qatar.

THE FAVOUR

It was lunchtime by the time Mike got off the plane at Heathrow. He had managed to get a lot of sleep in the eight-hour flight from Doha and had eaten breakfast an hour before the final approach. The business class passengers were first off the plane, shooting down the familiar causeways of Terminal 5. Passport control had the eGates operating and he was only momentarily held up by the dregs of the previous flight. He went straight downstairs to the baggage claim area to collect his bag and head to the Heathrow Express. He had some e-tickets left over on his phone from when he'd bought a bulk load on his last intensive travel engagement. There were a few minutes before the train left so he headed down towards the middle carriages, operating on autopilot, dozens of trips to and from Heathrow instilling in him the knowledge of which door opened closest to the ramp at Paddington. That ramp would take him to the underground lines and then to his old office. He remembered a time when the automatic ticket gates hadn't been there so, if you managed to make the twenty minutes to London before the conductor could get to you and process the electronic ticket, you effectively travelled for free. Always a fun game in a crowded train, trying to estimate whether the conductor would get to you in time. Because of that, he loved the tourists who hadn't obtained a ticket prior to travelling or who had some burning question that only the conductor could answer. All great delays and contributing to free rides for Mike.

As they pulled into Paddington, Mike finally remembered that he wasn't going back to his office and that he needed to catch a bus to Kings Cross for a train to Cambridge. He got his bag and pulled away from the main streams of passengers in order to work out his route. Ideally, he would have been at the front of the train but never mind. He walked half the length of the train, through the ticket machines at the end and out of the station into a balmy London early summer afternoon. The tight streets near the station were bustling with tourists, business travellers and local office workers getting lunch. The chaotic crowding was in marked contrast to Auckland with its wider footpaths and fewer travellers. Mike realised that he wasn't being very fair with his comparison—he'd mainly seen the streets of Auckland after rush-hour had abated.

The bus wasn't full but it was still awkward with his suitcase. He managed to get it into the reserved area just behind the driver's cubicle, lucky that no parent with a buggy or disabled passenger in a wheelchair had commandeered it. Twenty-five minutes later, he exited right onto the plaza outside Kings Cross and entered the huge semi-circular, sail-like concourse. Mike stood with fellow travellers peering up at the electric boards displaying the different trains, their departure times and platforms and intermediate stations. He got out his phone and did a search from Kings Cross to Cambridge and then checked the departures board. While the boards were correct most of the time, he'd sometimes made the mistake of getting on the first train out of the station rather than waiting for the quickest train for his destination then enduring a full hour stopping at every intermediate station when he could have waited another few minutes and boarded the express. So he made a habit of double-checking that the next train was the best train to catch. The journey details matched with what was on the boards so he went to the ticket machine to get his ticket. Ten minutes later he was pulling out of King's Cross, heading north.

He hadn't yet had a chance to sit down and have a quiet reflection on what he'd learned from Svetlana. The hour trip to Cambridge would be ideal. He didn't need that long though—apart from the photo he'd taken of the conversation with her lover, and that her "agent" in Sydney was called Dimitri, he didn't have much to mull over. Maybe he could find out her phone number based on the screenshot. A colleague, Todd, had been on an engagement that had relied on proving that a specific person had been travelling between London and a country in the Middle East on particular dates. What a lot of people don't realise about cell phones is that all the time they're turned on they are in constant contact with the cell towers all around them—regularly pinging them to find the tower with the best signal, so that if the one closest to you is overwhelmed with traffic, then one a little further away is the one used for calls. Then, as the traffic reduces on the closer one, it becomes the one with the strongest signal and therefore takes over as the preferred one. All these pings are recorded by the cell tower, but the length of time the information is stored differs by phone company and country. The colleague had explored options to gain access to those tower records. Once they had them they would be able to say that the suspect definitely was in the country in question. The UK based tower data required a court order but it only took a call to the right person in the Middle Eastern country to gain access to the records of the cell phone tower in that country.

Mike got out his phone and rang Todd. He answered on the first ring. "Hi Mike, thanks for getting back to me." Mike was puzzled but didn't interrupt. "Here's my problem. There's an issue with the search function on the site and the three guys keep kicking it around blaming the others, and I need to know whose fault it is so I can be decisive and fire someone. You know, new CEO, show them all I mean business. But I don't know enough about the technical side and obviously can't ask them."

Mike had no idea what Todd was talking about but thought it would make it easier to ask for a favour if he gave a favour first, so he switched to consulting mode to find a solution. Actually, not consulting mode—that involved talking slowly and asking for unneeded background information to increase the billable time—instead he focused on the task at hand.

"OK, tell me about the site, what are you searching for? Is the search totally broken?"

"As I said in my message, I'm the new CEO for a tech startup booking tradesmen onto jobs. The search is for a plumber, say, to find all his jobs. For lengthy searches it works fine, it's only when the search is for the one day that it doesn't bring back any data. And, as you can imagine, the ability to see all the jobs for today would be kind of handy, right?"

Mike suspected he knew what the issue was.

"And who are the guys kicking the blame around?"

"Grant is our test lead, Barry is the database guy and Colin is the BA."

"And does Grant have test scripts and results?"

"Yeah, but his scripts are all about how the site performs under load."

"OK, so who coded the site? Who wrote the search code?"

"Barry wrote the search but he's saying that he just followed what Colin said to do."

"And what does Colin say?"

"He can't understand why it doesn't work"

"OK, here's what I want you to do. Ask Barry for a list of all the data on a spreadsheet. Then ring me back."

"Sure. Thanks, Mike!"

A few minutes later Todd rang back. "OK, now what?"

"Choose one of the days which should have data."

"OK."

"Now put that date into the search. Just that date for both the start and end of the range."

"OK. Nothing is coming back."

"Good. Now make the end date of the search the day after you've got at the moment."

"So from today to tomorrow? OK. Ah! There are those appointments."

"And are there any appointments in the spreadsheet for tomorrow?"

"Yes, but they're not showing up. I'd expect them to be showing up."

"Here's what is happening. In the database you're storing the appointments as what is called a datetime—the date with the time bolted on the end. And that makes sense, right? But the dates being passed into the search are just the date part."

"So? I only want to see today's appointments. I don't want to specify the times or have those in the search. The UI is cluttered enough as it is."

"Yup I get that. The issue is that the database is adding a time to the date itself behind the scenes. It's interpreting the datetime as being midnight of the day that is provided. So if you give it today's date to search then it is trying to find appointments between midnight tonight and midnight tonight. Which is zero appointments. The search I asked you to do, which did bring back data, was interpreted as 'show me the appointments from midnight today to midnight tomorrow'. And that brought back the results you originally wanted but not what you thought you were going to get."

"OK, I think I follow. So how do I fix it and who do I fire?"

"Tell the database guy to manually append '23:59:59' to the end date. Or make the search end date the day after that which is provided. Either way. Or ask the database guy which one he wants to do."

"Whose fault is this?"

"Yours."

"Huh?"

"OK, not yours. But whoever hired these guys. I'm assuming they're all from big firms? They don't think like startup employees. They seem to be concentrating on just their job or, worst case, on one little part of their job, which is what you expect when you're in a big team. And you're going to have this sort of thing again in the future. Look, the database guy blindly coded something which he should have realised was rubbish. He should have been more critical of the spec. The BA framed his logic poorly, I'm guessing. He probably wrote something like 'bring back results between start date and end date' without spelling out exactly what that meant at a detailed level. And the tester was too focused on the site performance under load instead of checking that the search actually worked. You won't be able to fire them, but they're not a good fit."

There was silence on the other end of the phone as it sunk in. "Thanks, Mike. Appreciate it."

"Before you go, I've got a favour to ask of you," interjected Mike.

"Sure, anything."

"Do you remember the Middle East job with that trafficker?"

"Project Balsa? Sure."

"You were exploring ways of getting access to cell tower records and I know you ended up getting the court order in the UK and reaching out to the royal family in the Middle East, but what other ways were you exploring getting that data?"

There was another pause. "OK, I guess I can dig out the guy's details. There are some... let's call them interesting people... around the world who deal in this sort of thing. Hit and miss depending on how accessible the data is. We had no luck in either jurisdiction, but you might have better. It's not for the UK is it?"

"I'm really not sure—probably not."

"OK, it's just that the guy was useless for that. I'll send it to you. As I say we didn't end up using him, so I don't know if he's legit or not. Thanks for your help!"

As soon as Mike hung up the call, he checked his voice messages. Sure enough, there was the one from Todd, apparently left yesterday. Strange that he hadn't received any notification when he'd turned his phone back on after the flight.

True to his word, Todd sent the email details through for his contact straight away. Now Mike had to think about what data he needed. He figured that Svetlana would have turned her phone off sometime before take-off, so he'd be looking for a cell tower at Sydney airport at say 9:30pm, 15 minutes before they took off. At Doha airport he figured she would have turned her phone back on straight after landing, so call it 5:20am, 15 minutes after landing. He completed his email to the mystery contact, identifying that he was interested in cell tower records for the two airports with the dates and times involved.

He looked at his watch and swore. They'd be in Cambridge shortly. He packed up his laptop and collected his luggage from the racks, giving the SD card a final pat before heading to the door to wait for the train to arrive at the platform.

THE DROP OFF

Mike went over the plan in his mind. He'd just arrived in Cambridge and was walking through the station. He would head to the home of Heath Cox and see who opened the door. If it was a low-browed neanderthal with muscles, tattoos and a thick Russian accent, he would explain that he was the neighbour and just wanted to borrow a cup of sugar. If it was a slim, short guy with a closely cropped beard, then he would hand over the SD card. He absentmindedly passed through the ticket gates on autopilot, the orange card ticket disappearing into the machine. Then, he thought, he'd wait while they crunched the data. Presumably, after they found evidence of the satellite they would know what to do. Was there some sort of Satellite Police? The Americans had their new Space Force, maybe they would have some interest? Anyway, it would be off his plate by then. Gavin would find some comfort and Gary would find some peace.

His phone's map told him the way and he blindly followed the route it brought up. Apparently, a fifteen-minute walk. He turned over in his mind what would happen should they have proof that there was a satellite in the sky robbing a small population in a small country in the South Pacific from watching some weird sport. It really didn't feel like the sort of thing to make an international incident about.

He was beginning to feel overdressed. It was overcast but there was still significant heat in the air—a little too warm to be hauling a wheeled suitcase around the footpaths of Cambridge. He kicked himself. He should have found a left luggage locker at the station.

He made his way through the quiet back streets of the university town, his route not taking him anywhere near the picturesque old buildings but wending its way through nondescript suburban streets which could have been anywhere. The street which matched the address he'd been given was a cul-de-sac. The numbering of the houses threw him a little—so much so that he had walked past the apartment block matching the numbers before he realised it. He stopped on the other side of the road to check the map on his phone and finally realised which building was the one he wanted, one block over and on the other side of the road. It had a frosted glass door on the ground floor, guarded by an intercom, and above that was a staircase heading up four floors, the glass of the floor to ceiling windows totally clear—which was fortunate, because a man was standing on the stairwell peering out the window, his hands on the bannister. Occasionally he would turn nervously to look up the staircase, before turning again and inspecting the street. It was hard to say how tall he was, but he was definitely in good shape. Clean-shaven though.

It was impossible to know if he was being paranoid or justifiably cautious when acting on the internal alarm bells that occasionally rang in his head, but Mike was a great believer in trusting his gut, even if that made him look foolish. This time he made sure the man on the stairs was looking away and then headed back towards the main road where he had passed a newsagent on the way in. The aisles were too narrow for his suitcase but he was lucky that they had SD cards for sale behind the counter. Twenty quid later he was throwing the plastic wrapping into the bin outside the shop and retracing his steps.

As soon as he'd placed his hand on the intercom to buzz the apartment number he'd been given, the man he'd seen on the stairs came down and opened the door. The guy was about the same height as Mike and definitely not slim—he had good muscle tone, carried himself easily and moved fluidly. He greeted Mike by name with a distinct English accent, introducing himself as Heath Cox and that he would have to excuse him as he was just heading out on a very important errand. Would he be able to give him the SD card now?

Mike stood with the newly bought SD card in one hand and the handle to his suitcase in the other, wondering how he could trick the man into confirming that he wasn't actually Heath. Warmly he returned the greeting, shaking the man's hand while retaining the SD card in his left hand. "Really great to meet you, Heath. Wow, you've shaved! Almost didn't recognise you there. How long did your beard get before you decided to shave it off?"

The man was momentarily thrown before recovering. "Oh, yes of course. It was quite long, probably down to about here," he said, gesturing a little ambiguously, but sufficient to confirm it wasn't 'closely cropped'.

"Ah, yes. Well if you have to rush off, here's the SD card. Anything you can tell me would be brilliant." The man didn't quite snatch the card out of Mike's hand but it wasn't far off. Then he was striding away. Mike watched him hurry around the corner in the opposite direction that he'd come from. A few minutes later the sound of a car driving off at some speed filled the quiet suburban streets.

Mike took a second to catch his breath, and then returned to the intercom and buzzed the apartment number he'd been given. "Hullo?" came the response.

"Heath, it's Mike. We've been exchanging emails?"

"Ah yes, I'll pop down."

The real Heath Cox was shorter and slimmer than the imposter and sported a very thick beard. Mike told him about the other man and Heath was shocked.

"I'm shocked. Shocked, Mike. What could possibly be on the card which would provoke such subterfuge? Come on, let's go to my lab so we can see what's on it." He gestured to Mike's suitcase as they walked away from the apartment. "You probably didn't need to bring that many clothes. It'll only take a few hours to crunch the data and see what's on the card."

Mike started to explain that it was because he'd come from New Zealand when he saw the corner of Heath's mouth twitch and realised he was having a joke at Mike's expense.

"Here we go," Heath said as they turned the corner. They stood in front of a generic low-slung, two-storey office block. Heath touched a key fob to the black box beside the door and they went inside. They were in some sort of biomedical wing, with labs interspersed with offices, nobody around.

"Where is everyone?" asked Mike.

Heath gave him a confused look before shrugging. "It's Saturday, plus the semester finished like six or seven weeks ago. The only people here would be the odd PhD student or maybe someone catching up on some research."

They continued down the hallway and into an office. It was decorated in a weird combination of medical pictures of eyes and posters of constellations, with plaster models of eyeballs on bookshelves. Heath rolled up to the desk on an office chair and turned on a computer on the desk under a large flatscreen monitor. Mike looked at some of the decorations and posters before calling over his shoulder to Heath. "You must spend all your time either looking through a microscope or a telescope, right?"

Heath looked back as if considering this for the first time. "I guess so, hadn't thought about that at all. Do you have the data?"

Mike handed over the SD card and watched as Heath plugged it into the PC. Heath copied the data files over to a folder on his PC and then opened up one of them, maintaining a muttered commentary as he did so. "So what have we got here... OK... Video files... ah good, telemetry... so... nothing happens... hmmm.... That's a long file. And the other one... OK, same spot..."

Heath turned to Mike. "So there's a huge amount of data here and I'm not going to watch the days and days of data to see where anything actually changes. You're lucky we had a PhD who was doing Data Science write us a program especially for these tasks."

"What do you mean?" asked Mike.

"We were watching the effects of certain formulations of serum on the cells in an eye and we needed to know precisely when the chemicals started to have an effect. So we managed to obtain a high-speed camera that took thousands of frames per second and set it recording. That was great because we could zoom right in to where we needed to see, but it was bad because we had so much video footage of the same spot. So we got Nikki to build a program that took the video and identified when the image changed, with a nice buffer there in case the image moved for whatever reason. Quite sophisticated. Anyway, I feel certain I can use it here to see when there were changes in the video. Let me load it up. It doesn't have a nice interface or anything, so you have to know how to set it up using code. This might take a while. There's a kitchen down the hall if you'd like a cup of something."

"Can I get you anything? Tea?"

"Yes, thanks, that would be great—white, no sugar."

Mike headed down the hall and found the kitchen which turned out to be more of a kitchenette with a microwave, a hot water cylinder and a fridge and some passive-aggressive signs taped to the wall. "I'm not your mother, tidy up after yourself," was Mike's favourite. He found the mugs and a large box of tea bags and gave the milk in the fridge a sniff. Two minutes later he went back to the office, a mug in each hand. Heath was concentrating on what was on his screen, so Mike put the mug down beside the keyboard and nudged his arm to show him it was there. Heath grunted an acknowledgement and returned to the task at hand. Mike found a visitor's chair and sat on it, marvelling at the difference between a real scientist's office and ones he'd seen in the movies. In the movies, you would have a window with some sort of view, and the office would be big enough to have a couch of some description where he'd be able to wait in comfort. In reality, there were no windows and a flickering fluorescent bulb, with barely room for the two chairs, bookshelves and desk.

Mike was still in the unnatural awakened state he knew well from his work travels. The brain realised its internal clock was misaligned from what the sun was telling it—it had had some sleep, but barely enough. Eating breakfast before arriving into London after having had no food on the previous leg of the flight had been a good idea. Food tended to anchor the circadian rhythm. It was like the first hit of coffee after being up for a day. The brain was clear and the need for more sleep was just in the background nagging, but you just knew once the caffeine wore off you'd be struggling to string two thoughts together and holding eyelids open with matchsticks.

The tea was helping. He watched over Heath's shoulder as he finished making some changes to some sort of settings file, before trying a few times to set the process running. Various error messages popped up, indicating a less than perfect setup before Heath tracked down the steps required and completed the setup to the program's satisfaction. And then the screen was filled with a constant stream of rolling green on black text with status and percentage complete notifications counting up slowly. Heath leaned back and sipped his tea, not commenting on the temperature of the liquid, which must have been tepid at best by now. They watched the updates flash across the screen in companionable silence, until the numbers all ticked over to 100%.

Heath turned to Mike. "Shall we see what Gavin found?"

Mike nodded.

As Heath navigated through the folders on his PC, he kept a constant commentary. "Gavin recorded the same spot on the night sky for a month, the telescope turning off when the amount of light coming through the aperture was too much for the sensor. There were five instances of that spot in the sky changing and one of those was very fleeting, so I think it might have been a seagull or something—it was one or two frames at most. But these four instances are very interesting." He had navigated to a new folder the program had made with the five video files, one noticeably smaller than the other four.

"The resolution is not the best. Gavin... I won't waste your time with technical details, but his telescope isn't the best. I'm not a snob but... Anyway, it is what it is. And here is what we can see."

Heath maximised the video. The screen showed three stars, bright against the space behind. A second later they moved smoothly off the screen and instead they were now looking at a cube, end on, with a round aperture pointing directly at them. Heath moved closer to the screen, fixated on what they were seeing. "Oh my God, he was right. What the fuck is that?"

It was on the screen for all but a few seconds, then the stars swung back and the video ended. This was repeated on all the four videos. The duration the satellite was visible was different each time, but always less than five minutes.

"What time was it each time it opened?" asked Mike. "I want to see what TV program they wanted blocking."

Heath turned towards him and shook his head. "It's not the same time and day each time. It's different."

"Huh?"

"Unless they're moving the program around the schedule, they're not trying to block a TV broadcast. It looks more like they're trying to test the operations of the camouflage and the blocking system."

"What can you tell me about the satellite?"

"Well, I'll have to try to zoom in and see if I can clean up some of the footage, but it definitely looks like the same size of a satellite we lost track of after deployment last year."

"How do you lose track of something in the sky when everybody is looking at it?"

"Well, we can track things when we can see them but, unlike here on earth, that's actually only at night time. So if a satellite decided to move during the day we might not detect exactly where it ends up. Plus, last year the Russians put some satellites up in orbit that behaved very weirdly. There was a collision and that left a debris field which took a while to clear. Everybody was focussing on that debris, and it's possible it was just a screen for the sneaky satellite to change orbits and position. And then cloak itself. And especially if that was over the Southern Hemisphere, then who cares, right? What's down there? The South Africans got rid of their nuclear arsenal, and there's nothing else down there to justify that deployment of resources. But if it was testing manoeuvring and operational capabilities, then it's ideal—you practice out of the public eye and then move to where you need to be when you're ready to go."

"You said that the four unveilings were not regular—when was the last one?"

"Three weeks ago."

"And how long would it take to move from that spot of sky to something over the Northern Hemisphere?"

"Hard to know without more information about the propulsion system, most satellites don't move much because fuel is expensive and you want to maximise your payload rather than manoeuvrability."

"But it could get here in that time?"

"Oh definitely—that's not far to go at all."

"So what can it do? Gavin said that it frizzled the satellite TV. But that sounds like it would just be used for one satellite TV provider to take out his opposition. How much would that be worth to someone? Enough to justify the costs involved with putting that into orbit?"

"Well, depending on the strength of the signal, it might be able to block all receivers of the satellite signals in a small area, but that would be pointless because other receivers could pick up the signal and it wouldn't matter if the one you're blocking couldn't."

"So if that happened in Auckland, if there was another dish looking at the satellite then they'd be able to pick up the signal. So that could work there—only one dish in Auckland, overwhelm the signal and nobody gets TV?"

"Yeah, but if you're worried about that happening in the Northern Hemisphere it would never work, there are so many satellite dishes up here. There would always be another dish picking up the signal. Unless... unless they weren't trying to overwhelm the receiving dish but were bombarding the satellite with something which made it temporarily unable to transmit. That would make a black hole for the satellite. Not a problem for communications because they have built-in redundancy—they bounce signals between themselves all the time. But, for services requiring an overhead satellite-like navigation, that could be problematic. Or aerial photography, but who cares if Google doesn't have a recent photo for Google Maps, right? Who cares if the hotel is showing as a building site? They'll get another picture next week or next month or next year."

Mike thought for a second. "What do you know about intelligence satellites? Like spy satellites?"

Heath saw what he was getting at straight away. "Oh! Yes! That black hole would apply to spy satellites as well. Oh! So a sneaky satellite can hide what's going on from other people in a physical area, even if they have spy satellites."

"How big of an area would that cover?"

"I'm guessing an area a bit larger than New Zealand."

"The United Kingdom is pretty much exactly the same size as New Zealand."

"Ah, OK. So that would mean that the satellite would be able to make the whole of the UK a black hole to spy satellites. And potentially navigation too. That's a bit concerning."

Mike looked at him sideways. "That's an understatement. Could you send that video to the others in your network?"

"Sure, it's small enough. Why's that? Are you worried that something will happen to it?"

"Well, someone lurking outside your apartment was willing to pretend to be you to try and get the raw footage. And someone killed Gary because they thought he was Gavin—the guy who found the satellite in the first place." He didn't mention Svetlana. "So I rather think that there is a little danger to having the data you've got there. If more people have the data then hopefully that will make you and me less likely to be killed."

Heath smiled evilly. "Or just make it more of a bloodbath if they kill everyone that receives the data."

Mike rolled his eyes. "Well, we're hoping that doesn't happen obviously!"

"So what happens now?"

"I'll let you figure out what you can about the actual satellite, who made it, how it got there, that sort of thing."

"Sure, I can call in some favours from the others and see what we can come up with. But what are you going to do?"

"With the satellite data? Nothing. That's in your hands. Actually, is it possible to verify the satellite's existence from one of the other guys in the Southern Hemisphere?"

"It should be—geo is out thirty-something thousand kilometres from the surface of the Earth so Maggie in Oz should be able to see it if it's still there."

"Why do you say that? Why would you think it's moved?"

"Well, the last time Gavin saw it was three weeks ago, and you mentioned that there wasn't much down there to see. Plus if it is the satellite that we lost track of, then I figure they sent it down under for testing, and now it's coming back to actually perform whatever operation is required. I must admit it's all very exciting."

"So if it's not in the Southern Hemisphere I guess that would be important to know."

"Yeah, I guess. So do you want to give me your phone number and I'll give you a ring when and if I find anything? Or just email it to you?"

"Yeah, here you go." Mike gave him the number and then stood up, stretching. "I should probably head off. Can I get you to send me the snippets of the movies with the shielding removed? Just in case I need it. Would be great to have it to hand."

"Of course. How are you getting on with jetlag?"

"It hasn't hit yet—hoping to get home before it does! Speaking of which, I should probably head off. Last thing I want is to have a meltdown on the train."

With that, Mike collected his suitcase and made his way back to the train station, avoiding Heath's street, just in case the faux-Heath had returned clutching the empty SD card and wanted retribution. From there, the connection to High Wycombe took him back into the City and a pair of subway lines before a train got him home. All the way he was cursing himself for not going home first and dropping off his suitcase. The trains weren't necessarily bad but the tube system wasn't really built for the awkwardness of his luggage. He was glad he had packed light, so he was able to muscle the suitcase over barriers and up and down stairs without breaking stride. He was entering the latter half of the second hour, sitting in comfort staring out of the train window at the countryside of Buckinghamshire when his phone rang. He sighed and answered it.

"Hello, Mike? Heath here. I've had some responses from the team and we've had some success in identifying the satellite. It looks like it was the one that disappeared at the same time as that debris field appeared. It's not a design that we've seen before and the best guess is that the aperture is hiding a narrow beam weapon that will bombard the target with a broad spectrum of waves, mainly in the microwave range, so that it looks to all intents and purposes like sunspots are causing the outage."

"Ah, thanks for that. Good work! No sign of the satellite in the Northern Hemisphere?"

"Well, now we know what we're looking for, we'll definitely keep an eye out. But there is a lot of sky, so it might take a while to find, especially with that mirror being so dark—hard to detect against the black of space, right?"

"Yeah, I understand. Could you let the network know to be careful—someone was already killed for this information so if they decide to start cleaning up loose ends there's a bit of danger there. You especially, OK?"

"Sure, I'll pass it on, but the cat is out of the bag now. I'm not sure who we would tell though. It's a bit circumstantial—if the satellite was still over New Zealand then it may be worthwhile publicising but, with it gone, it just sounds..."

"A bit crazy?"

"Yeah."

"Yeah I know what you mean. Oh well, stay safe and if you find anything do let me know."

"Will do. Thanks, Mike."

A half hour later, Mike was slipping between the sheets on his own bed and sinking into a deep sleep.

THE MYSTERY

When he woke up, The Broker had responded to his data request. He had to read it twice to make sure he was reading it right because the contents were so surprising. The Broker said that he could get the data that Mike was looking for but, while the Doha airport tower logs could be had for the bargain-basement price of US$1,000, the ones for Sydney would be significantly more expensive. Not only that, The Broker would not be able to give a quote for just how expensive and would need a holding deposit of US$50,000 to even start exploring the options. That sounded like nothing short of an effort to extort money and Mike was close to hitting delete and forgetting all about it. The Doha amount was equivalent to £730—roughly the cost of a high-end smartphone. Not the sort of money Mike wanted to spend on an exploratory amount of data that would probably prove a dead-end—or the start of a trail costing more and more money.

Mike mulled it over while he showered. His body was telling him that, despite the full eight hours of sleep he'd managed overnight, he was still about ten hours short of catching up. He turned the heat up and had a good soak, dried off and got dressed. The visit to the kitchen for breakfast proved futile. He'd known that he would be away for a long time so had ensured that there was no milk in the fridge to go off or bread in the cupboard to go stale. He had been pretty sure that he'd remember to get breakfast supplies on the way home at the end of his holiday but with the adventures he'd had, it had completely slipped his mind.

He headed out the door to the local supermarket, returning half an hour later with a pantry full of groceries. Time spent mulling over the situation had persuaded him that purchasing the data was something he simply had to do. He'd had a breakfast muffin from the local Greggs, a belly full of bacon and eggs, plus a full night's sleep and a hot shower—all of which made him feel positive about moving forward.

He still needed reassurance that he wasn't getting scammed. If Todd had ended up using the source himself, or knew someone who had, that would make a difference. He rang Todd.

"Hey, how'd you get on with that search issue? How come you had the meetings on a Saturday?"

"Oh, we're in crunch time—seven days a week leading up to the launch. But yeah, the meetings? Great, just great. Barry wants to sue for a toxic work environment while Colin has taken out a personal grievance against me because he thinks I'm discriminating against him, and I'm not kidding here, for not having any children."

Mike grinned. "That's rough. Hey, I'm just doing some due diligence on your data broker. The data I want is going to cost a bit less than a grand but I obviously don't want to give that sort of money to some random person without proof that they're not going to run off. How did you find him?"

"Oh, sorry, I should have said—he came with some good recommendations. The Moscow office had used him on some investigation. You have to worry about evidentiary rules if you use anything in court—chain of evidence and all that—but it's all solid, so it should advance your case."

"Thanks, that's all I need."

"Great, I've got a call with the lawyers in half an hour. Speaking of which, when do you start your new job?"

"I think we're down to two months."

"Cool. Well, stay in touch."

"Laters," said Mike, hanging up.

He put through the money before he could overthink it, sending screengrabs of the proof of payment screen to The Broker's email address. He didn't know how long it would take for the data to come through, so he resolved to get on with his life. The satellite thread had come to a dead-end and there wasn't anything he could do until the data came through. Worse still, there was nothing he would be able to do if the data also ended up being a dead-end.

That afternoon he received a dump of data from The Broker. It was a list of cell phones that had connected to the cell tower around the time he had given. As he had expected for an airport, there were a lot of different nationality's cell phone numbers there. Then it hit Mike. He didn't know if Svetlana would have an Australian number, a Russian number or maybe even a cell phone which had been bought in the Middle East. He had a lot of data but no way of winnowing it down to the nuggets of gold that he was looking for.

He put his analytical hat on and thought it through. The data he had received didn't look like it included all the pings—the handshake connections which established which tower would be used for connecting should a call come in. He looked more closely. Maybe the data was actually helpful. It included the duration of the calls made that were routed through the towers—actually an amalgam of a variety of towers. The different columns corresponded to the calling number, the receiving number, the code for the tower used, the time the call started and the duration in seconds. A flash of anger went through Mike. This was not what he thought he had been buying. If Svetlana didn't use her phone, then this was useless. He needed every cell number in the airport, not just those that had made a call. He started to write a poisonous email to The Broker before stopping himself. It would be great to vent but that wouldn't get him anywhere. And how would a list of cell numbers three or four or a hundred times longer than the one he had help?

No, he had to assume that Svetlana would be on the phone as soon as she was through the air bridge and into the lounge. Or through passport control into the city, if her cover story about the modelling was true. So he dug into the data. Mike was not surprised that, for a plane coming in from Australia, there was a spike of Australian cell phones all calling around that time. There was just one Russian number making a call at that same time. One. No guarantee that was Svetlana but, if he could find out more, then he might be able to establish her phone number.

He sent The Broker an email thanking him for getting the data to him so quickly and asked what information he could provide about a Russian cell phone number.

I have access to a lot of data in Russia. What do you need?

He sent the Russian cell number and asked what kind of information could be provided based on that. He didn't have to wait long to find out.

For the person's name, date of birth, license plate, passport number for the cell phone number provided: ₽1,000 each. For the last three months call information (not message contents) for each person ₽5,000. For complete travel information for the past three months ₽2,000.

Sighing, Mike added it all up. ₽8,000. He had no idea what a ₽ was or how much it was worth, but a quick Google told him he was looking at a little more than £80. Not a lot compared to what he'd already spent, but he was acutely aware that it was starting to add up.

In for a penny, in for a pound, he thought. He made the payment and sent through the proof. An hour later he read his emails and a smile started to spread across his face and just wouldn't stop getting broader by the second. There on his screen was a passport photo of Svetlana. Like all passport photos, she looked more like a psychopath and less like the femme fatale she was, but it was definitely her. And her date of birth, all of her travel information and cell phone metadata. Who she spoke to and for how long and when. Success! Now all he had to do was to make sense of this great wad of data.

The next day, Mike's phone rang. The caller ID read "withheld". He answered, expecting a robocaller asking if he'd been in an accident that hadn't been his fault. Which was pretty much the definition of the word accident. So he rather testily answered the call with a "Yes".

A nervous-sounding voice on the other end of the phone hesitated before asking "Michael Reid?"

"I'm Michael," he responded.

"Michael, my name is Dan Robinson. I'm a private investigator and am investigating a case. Can we meet for a coffee?"

"What's this about?"

"I'd rather not talk about it over the phone but a friend in Russia indicated that we were looking for the same things."

Mike smiled. The cell phone lead looked to be sprouting. Very fortunate, because that was the only lead he had. Still, caution was required here. Extreme caution after his experiences with Svetlana and the fake Heath. It seemed he had the upper hand for the first time since this whole thing began. Time to take advantage.

Two hours later, Mike was soaking in a Jacuzzi in his local gym, overlooking the pool. An overweight middle-aged man walked in from the changing rooms, his eyes ringed by dark circles. He had a receding hairline and a pelt of dark hair on his chest and back. He walked awkwardly on the concrete floor, throwing his towel on a recliner near the pool, before ascending the ladder and flopping less than athletically into the hot water.

Mike reached over. "Dan? Mike."

Dan shook his hand grumpily. "Was the cloak and dagger stuff really necessary? I didn't need another pair of swimming trunks. If you'd told me

I'd need them, I could have brought mine."

Mike shrugged, his demeanour displaying a sullen disregard for Dan's suffering. Mike had requested that Dan meet him at the local coffee shop, but had kept a watchful eye from the other side of the street to ensure that there was no one else following him. Mike had rung Dan after he'd been waiting for five minutes and told him instead to go to the local clothing shop. He'd slowly walked behind, keeping an eye out for anyone who looked out of place before ringing and telling Dan to buy a pair of swimming trunks and then to meet him in the Jacuzzi at the gym. Mike figured if he was going to be poisoned then it would be difficult to administer the poison wearing swimming trunks and in a semi-public place. Especially with the girls from the coffee shop attached to the gym. They always tried to see him getting in and out of the pool or Jacuzzi, so they would also be witnesses in case Dan turned out to be some sort of assassin. Mike always allowed himself that moment of conceit. He worked hard on his body, it was nice to be appreciated for it.

"I am a cautious man." Mike smiled at him ruefully. He'd missed out on potentially free sex with a very high-class prostitute out of fear of being assassinated, so he was going to put his new friend Dan through his paces before deciding whether to trust him. "You mentioned that we wanted the same things. I'm curious as to what they are."

Dan held up a finger. "I said we are looking for the same things. Information on the same people."

"Ah, Lana and the guy she was seeing—Gabe?"

Dan nodded. "So what's your interest in them?"

Mike grinned. "You called me. You have to give to get."

A look of annoyance flashed across Dan's face. After a second, he leaned back into the hot water and sighed.

"Gabe was a customs agent at Felixstowe. He died recently. The police ruled it a suicide but the widow wasn't convinced, so she hired me to investigate. We got his cell phone records but it didn't match with what was on his phone. All the messages to a particular number had been deleted. It was a Russian number and I had a couple of contacts over there, so I reached out for more information. Apparently, that was very close to the time when you asked for exactly the same information."

Mike wondered how much he should share. "So what do you know about Svetlana?"

"Very beautiful, Russian national. Late 20s, sometime model. There is some surveillance footage of her with Gabe and a lot of texts between them. Working hypothesis is that they were having an affair."

Mike was about to mention the text Svetlana had shown him, but Dan looked up and continued.

"Except her phone records are interesting. Tell me, Mike, are you any good at seeing patterns?"

Before he could stop himself, Mike blurted out, "It's how I make my living."

Dan eyed him for a second, obviously making a mental note, before continuing. "What do you do straight after calling your lover? If you're a sixteen-year-old girl you might ring a best friend to squeal and talk about it, but if you're a model in her late 20s, would you bother ringing or texting anyone? But straight after almost every phone call and text from Gabe, the lovely Lana texted or phoned a particular number. Not a Russian number, unfortunately, otherwise we'd be able to find everything about the person on the other end of those calls. No, this was a UK number. I'm calling him The Handler. It's a pity we can't get hold of the same data in this country, it would make investigations a lot easier."

Mike frowned. He'd heard the same arguments before. "Tell me, Dan, before the PI gig, did you work for the police at all?"

Dan shuffled uncomfortably, frowning. "I did, why?"

"No reason," replied Mike breezily. "So what do you think?"

There was a pause. "Have you seen a picture of Gabe?"

Mike shook his head.

"Have you seen a picture of Svetlana?"

Mike nodded, a smile flitting across his face.

"So there's a bit of... a discrepancy between the two, no? Gabe was in his fifties and the coroner said if he hadn't hanged himself the high blood pressure or diabetes would have gotten to him quite shortly. The guy at the corner shop where we got the video footage asked if Gabe had won the lottery when he saw them together."

"You don't believe that opposites attract?" Mike asked, just to be argumentative.

Dan didn't take the bait. "The coroner certified it as a suicide. He hanged himself in a hotel room in the centre of town. The maid found him. Nothing missing. No note. The video surveillance in the lobby shows him checking in, paying cash at 6pm. My working hypothesis is that Svetlana was sleeping with him to compromise him. Someone working with the customs inspectors at the country's busiest port would be a prime target for organised crime bringing drugs in or smuggling people into the country. When they tried blackmailing him, he wouldn't play ball and so they killed him before he could expose them. Dressing it up as a suicide. We figure the number she communicated with was her handler—The Handler. She takes her orders from them and reports in."

"No sign of who that is?"

Dan looked exasperated. "No, in fact the only clue came from our friend in Russia who asked if we wanted to talk to someone who was also looking for the same contacts."

"Hence this conversation. So let's say that you're right, that this was a..." Mike broke off as another gently overweight man started to clamber into the Jacuzzi. He noticed the pause in the conversation and the way both Dan and Mike looked at him, and reversed direction, slowly making his way to the pool instead. Mike waited until he was out of earshot. "So if someone wanted to arrange the import of something dodgy, how do we track her handler? Do you have any contacts who can get cell phone data here?"

"No, it's a little more difficult here. If we had a court order, then no problem but, as I said, the local police say this is suicide, therefore there's no way we could get them to ask a judge for a court order."

"What about your contacts in the local force? Is it worth sharing what we've got? Persuade them that it wasn't a suicide?"

Dan looked uncomfortable. "No, they've got the case all squared away and we won't be making any friends with our theories. So, I've given. What do you know?"

Mike ran through everything he'd found out.

"So what's our next move?"

"I've been working on one of the staff at the hotel to try and get access to the rest of the surveillance video. Just because nobody suspicious came through the lobby, doesn't mean there isn't a video of them getting in somewhere else. I guess until then we share what we find? And maybe not resort to amateur theatrics with Jacuzzis?" Dan finished with a grin.

Mike wasn't bothered. He stood up and stretched. "Will let you know if I find anything," he promised. He headed out to the changing room, showered and changed while lost in thought. On his way home, he wondered if he'd missed the connection between The Handler and Svetlana. Like any pattern, once you've had it pointed out it was obvious but he hadn't looked at the data through the lens of an engagement—it was too close for that, he didn't have the objectivity. He needed to take himself out of the investigation and approach it like any other case.

By the time he got home, he had a plan of attack. He laid out the events as explained by Dan and then started constructing a timeline of communication. He overlayed the international travel of Svetlana to the UK.

He categorised the contacts as "Gabe initiated" and "Svetlana initiated" and mapped out the patterns in communications. Sure enough, nine times out of ten when The Handler got in touch with Svetlana, there was a connection with Gabe straight away afterwards. About half the time Gabe got in touch with Svetlana there was a follow-up message sent to The Handler. He also graphed the times of the calls and messages from Gabe to Svetlana, along with the length of the calls. Nothing before ten each morning. Nothing between 6pm and 9pm each night. Keeping it from the wife.

He looked at when the calls and messages to Gabe had started and stopped. They'd begun about a week after Svetlana had arrived in London on the Aeroflot service from Moscow. But she'd gotten in contact with The Handler almost immediately after landing in London. It looked like the last contact she'd had with Gabe was an hour before he'd checked in to the hotel. And just before that was a phone call from The Handler. Then nothing for hours until a call from her number to an Australian number. In fact, that looked like when she'd arrived in Australia, as for a period all the incoming and outgoing calls were all to Australian numbers.

OK, so let's put our high-priced prostitute hat on, thought Mike. We have an agent called Dimitri who gets us jobs. He sends us to the UK for the Gabe job. But she'd arrived from Moscow. So did she live in Moscow or Sydney? Let's assume that she lived in Moscow. She gets the job and leaves for the UK. The Handler is in the UK and using a UK phone. So how did she know how to get in touch with him? Email? Maybe Dimitri gave her the contact details. So when would he have done that? Presumably sometime before she left the country. It might have been the last thing or the plans could have been made and communicated to her far in advance. No way of knowing. All he could do is maybe go through the contacts she'd been talking or texting to in... what, a month prior to coming to the UK? And see if any of them were suspicious. Or named Dimitri.

She was a popular girl. In the month before coming to the UK she'd talked or texted a total of 73 people. He thought about it. Could he bring that number down? Was there a likely time or frequency of contacts that would make the call stand out? Could he look at all the times the person had been contacted once and once only? Would the call be long or short? Text only or voice call as well? Or voice only? He couldn't think of any justification for any such rule, so totted it up. He was going to have to ask for the contact details of all 73. This was going to be expensive. Maybe he could negotiate a bulk discount?

A few email exchanges later he discovered three things. First was that his data broker in Russia didn't give discounts. He'd have to pay top dollar for the details of all 73 people. The second thing he discovered was that Svetlana partied a lot. He should have paid more attention to the times that the texts and calls had happened. On the plus side, if he ever ended up in Moscow, he had the beginnings of a very impressive little black book. Some of the photos provided by the data broker were just passport or driver license photos, but even those showed that the people Svetlana had been in contact with had been some of the most attractive individuals he'd seen. Male and female.

The third thing Mike discovered was that a week before Svetlana had left for the UK, she'd talked on the phone for two minutes with someone named Anatoly Maksutov. He turned out to be someone employed by the SVR which, after a brief Google search, turned out to be the foreign intelligence branch of the Russian government. Now that was a solid lead. It was unlikely that Anatoly was in fact Dimitry unless he was going deep undercover in Australia, posing as Svetlana's pimp. He had solid evidence linking Svetlana with Anatoly but still didn't know the identity of The Handler, the guy pulling the strings with Svetlana while she was in the UK. Mike was pretty sure that the guy had to be Russian, but had no way of proving that—it was just a hunch.

But he did have one way of trying to find him. Presumably, he would be able to connect The Handler to this Anatoly, so he got out his wallet yet again and asked for the call records for Anatoly's phone. He would have to spend more money on the passport records of each of his contacts but it would be worth it because one of them was bound to be The Handler.

What he found was distressing.

The list of whom Anatoly had communicated with in the week before Svetlana got the call from Anatoly only brought up twenty-three contacts and, after removing seven due to demographic reasons (children, the elderly, same surname), he had a solid list of contacts. When he ordered the passport details of each of them, he expected to see maybe one of them heading to the UK a little before Svetlana had left. That would be his Handler. Instead, he came up with ten of them heading to London on five different dates. "Two by two by two..." he thought as he gazed at the results of his data expenditure.

He thought back to the perpetrators of the 9/11 attacks on the World Trade Centre: four cells of four men each. Then to the Novichok attack on the Skripals by a pair of operatives. Something was coming and he didn't know what it was. But it was big. Well, bigger than the assassination of two people but presumably smaller than 9/11.

THE KINDLING

Mike knew better than trying to get anywhere with the Home Office through their public-facing phone numbers. His story wasn't sufficiently different from a conspiracy theory you would expect to hear from someone wearing a tinfoil hat and yelling that the microwave was listening to him. He checked his contacts to see if anyone who he had worked with in the past had decided to work for the government and was a little surprised when none had. Sure, a couple of his American colleagues now worked for the FBI, and some of his UK-based colleagues now worked for one or other of the financial regulators, but he would have expected through sheer weight of numbers that someone would have ended up in the agency responsible for keeping the nation safe. He snorted to himself. The premium that the financial services firms paid to ex-members of the regulators obviously didn't apply to the Home Office, so there was no point in the high achievers spending career time there.

If no one he knew actually worked there, he would have to canvas those who may know someone working there instead. He put feelers out amongst his network, wording the request in nebulous terms. He realised that if anyone from his contacts had joined MI5, then they would be less likely to update LinkedIn with their new job status.

His network came through eventually. Brian, who he'd worked with at his last job, had left to go into consulting and somehow been involved in a work capacity with someone from the Home Office. He was happy enough to share their name and contact details. Mike wasted no time in calling them. While hesitant on the phone, Sam Haley finally agreed to meet Mike after he managed to explain that what he had to discuss warranted a face-to-face meeting, and that the potential ramifications would be huge.

Mike prepared a document that walked the reader through the hypothesis that there was a concerted plot by ten Russians to import something illegally into the country. It included the dossier of cell phone records, a network diagram identifying how the individuals connected to each other, Mike's timeline of contacts between Svetlana and Gabe and a rather weak ending where the recommended course of action sort of trailed off. What was he expecting, he thought? Did he expect some sort of sting operation at the port? But without Gabe's involvement, the Russians wouldn't be able to get whatever they needed for whatever they were planning into the country. What then? A request to investigate every customs agent at every port in the country to see how many of them were potentially having an affair with a Russian? Tracking down the ten agents? No crime had actually been committed, Gabe's murder excepted—and that was being treated as a suicide. So he flipped through the document and considered his options.

"You're right about this being circumstantial. Without knowledge of what the ultimate goal is, it's a bit hard to stand here and tell you what we're dealing with. But the fact that they went to all the trouble of making Gabe's murder seem like a suicide, and that they sent Svetlana to have the affair with him to get some sort of access to the port surely is a cause of concern? That's a lot of resources in play. What would you expend ten agents on?"

"Thanks for bringing this to our attention sir, we'll make sure it's given the appropriate attention."

Mike knew when he was being fobbed off. Sam stood at the door, holding it open for him to leave. Mike sat in his chair for a second longer and then let out a sigh and placed his hands on his knees, ready to push himself up, ready to walk out of the interview room and down the hallway. Ready to head out of the building and to let the authorities take responsibility for investigating the Russians. But his inner sense of justice told him that this was wrong. That it wasn't fair on Gabe. Or Gavin or Gary. So he played the only card he had.

"I'm sure the press would be most interested in the story," he said softly. "Sure, getting a murder mixed up with a suicide only reflects badly on the local police, but once they find out Russians are involved and once they see a photo of Svetlana, I'm sure the story will get a lot of coverage. The press loves those full-page photos of pretty people on the front page. People will ask themselves, Who is protecting us from these foreign agents? And I'm sure that the memory of the Skripals being attacked on British soil without anyone in the intelligence services being any the wiser has left a lastingly foul taste. I won't be fobbed off."

There was a cold silence. "You do know that it is against the law to blackmail an officer of her majesty's government," Sam responded through clenched teeth.

Mike held his gaze. 'It shouldn't be necessary to blackmail someone to do their job."

The cold silence lengthened—eventually Sam told him to wait where he was and stalked off. The door closed behind him slowly on its own. There was a window in it allowing Mike to see the corridor outside. Sam returned a few minutes later, trailed by a middle-aged man of immediately forgettable features. Sam turned just before entering the room and spoke to the new guy. His face was turned away from the door so all Mike could see was the reactions on the new guy's face. It was quite the progression. At first shock—the guy even tried to interrupt with some words of protest. This didn't last for very long, as Sam cut him off. Next was confusion— Mike almost expected to see a giant yellow question mark appear over his head, like in a video game or comic. Then came some form of understanding, small nods of agreement. Finally some sort of determination set in, with a firming of the jaw and steeling of resolve as Sam finally opened the door and held it open for the new guy to enter. "Mike, this is Grayson. Grayson, this is Mike Reid. He has a dossier on the potential infiltration into the country of five teams of Russians which needs investigation. Please debrief him and open a case accordingly. You can rejoin the task force once that has been resolved." Sam stalked out of the room, leaving Grayson watching Mike.

"Is that the dossier?" he asked eventually, sitting opposite Mike.

"Yes," Mike responded, sliding it over. Grayson opened the cover and started to read through the documents.

"The thing about government work, and intelligence work in particular," Grayson started conversationally while running a finger down each page, "is that there is never enough time or resources to do everything that needs doing. So prioritisation decisions have to be made. Hard decisions. And that's when there aren't any emergencies going on. Events which require all resources to be working on the single most important thing to happen in recent history." He looked up, eyeing Mike over the top of his glasses. "And the public of the nation would be best served if we in the Home Office are able to focus on the things which we need to focus on." He went back to the dossier. He'd come to the page with the details of the ten agents. "And distractions like this one...." he trailed off into silence, gaze focused on the page. After a few seconds of thought, he got out his phone and sent a text. Then he turned to Mike, pulled out a pen and said "Tell me everything. Who are these men?"

Mike told his story as best he could, noting that Grayson's eyes betrayed particular interest in the mention of the customs worker at Felixstowe and of the satellite data. By the time he'd finished, he was starting to feel a bit hungry but was more curious as to what had changed the tone of the conversation, and how it fitted in with what else was going on. After divulging everything that he knew, he thought he might try and find out something from Grayson, seeing how he was obviously interested in what Mike had to say.

"So tell me—what are the Russians here for?"

Grayson had filled the spare whitespace on the backs of pages with notes as Mike had been telling his story. As the questions had petered out, he'd been reviewing what he'd written. He looked up at the question and peered over his glasses at Mike. This time he flashed a perfunctory smile that didn't touch his eyes. "Thank you for answering my questions, and for bringing this to our attention. You'll understand that I cannot discuss any investigation which is underway, so the most I can do is offer our thanks and take your details in case there are any follow-up questions," he said as he stood up and collected the papers together.

Mike didn't move. "Thanks for your time? I've spent upwards of £2,000 of my own money buying the data that made this case for you—which has proven very valuable to what is going on here and now.."—Grayson looked surprised at this—"and that's the thanks I get? I haven't even told you the most important part."

Grayson looked annoyed. "I'll remind you that it's a crime to withhold information pertinent to a case, Mr Reid. Especially when the safety of the country is at stake."

Mike looked bored. "Until you tell me what's going on, I'm happy to ask for a lawyer."

Grayson sat down with a sigh and rubbed his face. "First of all, we have wide-reaching powers to detain you without charge and without legal representation if we consider you a suspect under anti-terrorism legislation. Second of all..." he seemed to deflate in front of Mike. "Look, I've gotten maybe five hours of sleep in the last week. I don't need this shit. I'll tell you what's happening but you have to tell me everything you know, alright?"

Mike cocked his head and nodded. "Sure."

Grayson sighed again. "As a matter of course we monitor the

communication of fringe groups within the country—trade unions, anti-immigration, animal rights— anyone who might be tempted to take the step up from talking about action to actual violence. A couple of months ago some of the Communist groups at universities across the country started increasing the volume of their communications. The government was reducing Universal Credit with the aim of removing it entirely. The poverty groups and other social organisations increased their activities as well, so we thought the increase in Communist communications was related to that. More demonstrations, that sort of thing. It became clear that there was a concerted effort to grow membership on campus and a marked increase of fiery rhetoric. Again, easy for that growth to get lost in the general increase in activity as a result of the changes to Universal Credit.

"You remember the expenses scandal? The MPs found to be claiming that their moat on their ancestral home was a swimming pool so could qualify as essential exercise equipment. The vet's bills on two ponies were for their pet and therefore qualified for reimbursement as they were away from home for more than 90 days in the year. So those discoveries raised a certain level of antagonism among certain areas of the public. And the Communist groups began interacting more with a grassroots organisation called 'The 99%'. Same message, different audience. You wouldn't get support for the Communists from the working poor in the south, but they flocked to 'The 99%'. Same with the urban poor. The Communists stepped it up on campuses and the Trade Unions gained traction in the north.

"So all of a sudden we're getting bombarded with communications between these groups and within them as well. It's hard to cut through all the dreck and figure out who is pulling the strings."

"You think it's the Russians?"

Grayson paused. "No. There was some traffic referencing support from the Russians, but that came a long way into the build-up. This wasn't a plot organised by them. The only reference to the Russians indicated that there would be support landing in Felixstowe, which we interpreted as being an arms shipment. We had difficulty with the spy satellites over the area, which supports what you found out about the satellite situation—we've been denied eyes over our own country. But the name of one of the ten agents you identified matches a communique we received. He's been assigned a target on an estate in East Grinstead. The best we understand it, the ten agents haven't come over to lead any kind of insurrection. Apparently, in exchange for the arms, the organisers have been given lists of people of interest. It all looks like some sort of armed insurrection of incredibly wide scope and, under cover of this violence, the Russian agents will be given free rein to dispose of people they've deemed undesirable. The days of the Russians or the Soviets prompting armed uprisings are long gone, but they seem to be wanting to take advantage of the situation to place... a full stop in various people's life stories, shall we say?

"From what you've said, we don't know if they brought the arms through Felixstowe after all, or whether they had a backup plan in the same port, or a different one. But the Armed Forces are on notice, they've been briefed and we're trying to identify the ringleaders of the movement so that they can be arrested before the insurrection can get underway." Grayson closed his eyes and rubbed the bridge of his nose. "Now, what was the information that you were withholding?"

Mike pursed his lips. "Sorry, I didn't have any—I just needed to understand what was going on."

Grayson looked up and laughed almost manically. "Ah... Mike. Well played. Well, you have been very helpful. You've shone some light onto why we've not been able to get any satellite coverage which was keeping a lot of our boys up for many days, and the insights into the Felixstowe angle will undoubtedly lead further, so I guess I owe you one. I suggest you get some groceries and lock yourself inside for the next few days. You don't want to get caught up in all this."

Mike nodded. "Maybe I'll head to the South of France and wait it out there."

Grayson nodded. "Safer there. Go soon. Here's my card should you remember anything important. And Mike?"

Mike turned.

"Don't breathe a word of this to anyone. Under any circumstances. If I hear even a rumour that you've said anything to anyone I will have you locked up in a dark cell and the key thrown away sooner than you can blink. The last thing we need is panic."

Mike had just arrived home and was packing a bag when his phone rang. The caller ID recognised the caller as Reggie, the guy who had arranged his holiday in New Zealand.

"Hi, Mike, Reggie here. Hey, I just heard that you'd left the apartment in Auckland early, and I just wanted to make sure everything was OK, that the place was alright?"

"Hi, Reggie, thanks for calling. Yeah, the place was great, thanks. Loved the sauna—just what I needed!"

"Cool, I appreciate that the weather wasn't the best down there. The winters don't show the place in the best light, do they? Not like here—we had 30 degrees Celsius at the East Grinstead Summer Fete. I swear Mrs Somersby was going to faint."

"Ah, that's great. I'm sorry. Did you say East Grinstead, Reggie?"

"Yes, it's where we live. Eastwell Manor, East Grinstead in Sussex. Why's that?"

"Uh...is East Grinstead very big?"

"I don't know, I think it has about twenty thousand people in it."

"And how many estates would you say were there?"

"Ooh, I don't know about that—I'm sure there are maybe another ten or twelve large estates. Are you thinking of moving down here? It's quite commutable to London—half an hour into Victoria."

"No, that's fine. Thanks for that Reggie. And thanks again for the apartment— very much appreciated." Mike was torn. Grayson's warning was fresh in his ears, but Reggie had been very kind to him. Even the call would probably show up in the trawl of communications metadata. Probably flagging some sort of an alert for Grayson as they spoke. "Look I have to go, but you stay safe, OK?"

"Sure, you too."

Mike didn't know what to do. It had been simpler before Reggie's call. He was going to head to some villa overlooking the Cote d'Azur and soak up the sun until the country came to its senses.

But now he felt some kind of obligation to warn Reggie. He didn't know if Eastwell Manor was the estate where the Russian was heading, but it looked like he had a one in ten chance of being paid a visit once everything kicked off. And he didn't know what the insurrection would do. He presumed, if it was a communist uprising, then it would follow the same pattern for past revolutions: the property owners had their property confiscated and then were shot. The intellectuals and professionals—the lawyers, accountants and doctors—were lined up and shot. Anyone getting in the way? Lined up and shot.

Besides, weren't they square? Mike had done Reggie a favour, giving him the "Get out of jail free" card with HMRC, and Reggie had done Mike a favour with the apartment for a month. Mike stood staring at his suitcase sitting by the door waiting like a dog with his leash in his mouth.

He pulled Grayson's card out of his pocket and dialled the numbers.

"Grayson? Mike Reid here. When are things going to kick off? I think the Russian is going to go after my friend Reggie. Reggie Rutherford. It's Eastwell Manor, East Grinstead—if that makes a difference. No, no proof, but I've got to help him if I can and you said you owed me one."

There was a long pause while Grayson thought things through. "OK, listen I'll pull some strings for you. If you can get to Aldershot I can get you attached to the 1st Battalion of the Scots Guards who are our in-country assets in Sussex. They're based in the camp there. But this is at your own risk. I'll ring ahead."

HISTORICAL EVENTS

Mike sped down the M25 in his dark mauve BMW 3 series, ignoring road rules and speed limit. The traffic was lighter than expected, so he was making good time. Based on his conversation with Grayson, he had the name of one of the officers at Aldershot who could embed him with a unit of the Scots Guards based there. Just from his tone and terminology, Mike realised that plans had been put into motion and the country had already been apportioned to army units. That was promising, and maybe he would be able to get to Grinstead quickly. He would be at the mercy of whatever timetable the unit had been given to accomplish its goals, but with any luck they'd been told he needed to rescue Reggie and could make that a priority.

A half-hour later he entered Aldershot and made his way to where Google was telling him the barracks were. The street leading up to the barracks was cobbled with red bricks and lined with mature trees. Beside the road were various fields and obstacle courses and the occasional sign warning against stopping.

The road eventually ended at a car park just outside a guard post with its bright white barrier arms down and a soldier inside looking at him warily. As he approached the guardhouse, he noticed through the gate another soldier casually watching him while holding a rifle. The soldier in the guardhouse leaned over to the window. "Evening, do you have your papers on you?" Only his head was visible.

Mike shook his head. "A friend of mine at the Home Office said that you would be expecting me?"

"And your name would be....?" replied the soldier. He was wearing a drab khaki camouflage uniform with a khaki beret.

Mike told him and was asked for identification. He handed over his license and the soldier made an annotation on his clipboard. "Do you know the way?" Mike shook his head again. "Straight through the gate, second on the right," the soldier said, pointing. "Don't stray."

The gate opened and the soldier beyond stood to one side, levelling a gaze at Mike as he passed. To Mike's left were various large buildings and to his right was a large compound filled with a wide variety of vehicles, surrounded by an L shape of workshops and support buildings. It was an impressive site, encompassed by a chain link fence which was spotted with floodlights. Significant activity was occurring under the lights, with trucks being driven in or out of the workshops and men scrambling over or into them. Some of the trucks were drab olive and some a desert sand colour. The first turning on the right went straight into the compound but the second took Mike to a giant car park in front of a two-storey building. He pulled into a vacant spot and walked over to the entrance. A soldier was waiting there for him, greeting him by name. They walked together back the way Mike had driven—along the road back to the driveway which entered the truck compound. There they followed a path painted on the asphalt which moved at right angles towards the collection of trucks. The one they approached was surrounded by about ten soldiers in camouflage uniforms and helmets with straggly bits of cloth attached and wearing yellow wraparound safety glasses. They all carried rifles and had body armour on. One carried a spare blue helmet without the frizzy cloth on it and a blue armoured vest.

The truck looked like someone had taken a Land Rover and stretched the back chassis to add an additional set of wheels. Then they'd dipped the body in glue and driven through a fence, making it look like there was a cattle stop attached to each side and the front grill. Assorted lights and aerials were attached haphazardly and the exhaust came out of the engine bay like a snorkel and then ran along the top of the truck.

The soldier with the extra helmet and armour came over to speak to him.

"I'm Lieutenant Dan Smail. The Home Office has arranged for you to ride with us. We'll get you aboard in a few seconds, but just a few ground rules. Don't get in the way, don't touch anything and if the shooting starts and we're out of the truck, hit the ground. If we're in the truck stay in your seat and stay buckled up. Oh, and you're here at your own risk. Your insurance probably won't cover anything that happens to you, and you can't sue if anything goes wrong. That's pretty much it."

Smail's accent was more upper-class toff than Scottish, and Mike wondered if the unit name actually meant anything. They were at the rear of the truck by now, so there was a pause as Mike put the helmet and armour on, before one of the other soldiers gave him a hand up.

"I'm Private Andrews. This way to your seat. You're right behind the driving cab, so you might be able to see where we're going. You're last out when we deploy—first on, last off." This was more like it with Andrews' accent featuring the soft Scottish burr and rolling r.

Each of the seats was covered in a plastic bag. The two rows of seats followed the line of the interior walls of the truck, facing each other—five seats on the left-hand side, three on the right. A table of sorts stood between the rows near the front, directly below a hatch in the ceiling. Andrews helped him sort out his seatbelt which turned out to be a four-way harness secured in the centre.

"If we crash there's a cutter attached so you can cut your way clear, but the chances of that happening are pretty low."

The other soldiers had followed them in and were getting settled, securing their weapons with straps on the walls between the seats. The Lieutenant stood on the table between the seats in the back and his head and upper torso disappeared from view through the top hatch. Mike's immediate view was of the Lieutenant's groin. The rear doors closed with a clang and the cab rumbled to life.

There then proceeded about an hour of breezy driving down the major highways, the noise of the wind through the hatch competing with the engine noise. It was still possible to have something of a conversation and he caught wary glances from the soldiers periodically during their conversations. Andrews eventually asked the question that was on everyone's minds.

"So are you some sort of spy, sir?"

Mike was a little surprised. First of all, at the deference and being called 'sir' when he wasn't an officer. Then from a young white man, though he guessed if you were in the army you weren't necessarily one of the louts on the streets yelling obscenities or feeling threatened by a black man in a suit.

"Please call me Mike... I've been... helping out... with the Home Office." He was a little uncomfortable describing his relationship with the Home Office, which Andrews and the other soldiers misinterpreted.

"Does that mean you're MI6, sir?" Andrews persisted, obviously thinking that Mike's reluctance was due to his operating outside of the rules on a domestic case when MI6 were tasked with foreign intelligence.

"That's enough, Andrews," came a disembodied voice from the hatch.

"Ten minutes, chaps."

They were driving under bright lights and Mike assumed that was because they were in Grinstead, so he was a little surprised when the back doors opened and they filed out into the bright lights at the front of the terminal at Gatwick. Beyond the terminal, the early evening had taken the heat out of the day. They'd parked on the footpath outside the bus stops and there were a few startled looking passengers. A pair of police officers approached, with armoured vests over pullovers, peaked caps on their heads and each with a submachine gun on a strap pointing at the ground. The

Lieutenant went over to talk with them as the rest of the squad warily scanned the area, their own guns held at waist level with the muzzles pointed toward the ground.

Mike milled around with the other soldiers, looking confused. He thought they were going to Grinstead, but instead they had ended up at the airport. As the Lieutenant came back to rejoin them, he started walking towards him.

"I thought we were going to Grinstead," he said, trying not to let his impatience show.

"Slight change of plans. We have to wait here until the RTR rock up, then we head to Grinstead."

"RTR?"

"Royal Tank Regiment."

" Ah. When do you think that will be?"

"Oh, it should be tonight. They were a little slow getting away. Not all their guys received the recall notice before they took down the cell towers."

"Cell towers?"

"Yes, oh you didn't know? Your lot have taken down the towers to stop the other guys communicating."

Oh, thought Mike, that meant that he couldn't even warn Reggie.

"Ah, OK. So what do we do now?"

"Follow me, I only want to tell people once."

They headed back to where the squad were still standing.

"Listen up, chaps. We're to stand guard here until the RTR arrives, then we're heading further into West Sussex to start the roll-up. We're not expecting any trouble here but keep your eyes open. Two by two through the terminal. We've shared ops with the local police so check your targets. Comms on channel 3. Grantham, get your section some shut-eye. Take the Mastiff around the side and see if the sat link will work."

Mike spoke before he could stop himself. "There's a Russian satellite causing interference—spy satellites and comms will be out."

Lieutenant Smail stared at him for a second. "Grantham, try anyway, but reach out to the locals and see if we can patch into a phone line instead. We should be close enough to just use the VHF. While you're at it, see where the other two are, will you?" He strode back to the truck, and Mike exchanged glances with Andrews.

"We're left flank—our company has a total of six trucks and the others left before we did. They shouldn't have got lost and if airport security haven't mentioned them then something must have happened."

"Could they have gone to the wrong terminal?"

"Anything's possible," Andrews responded as he and one of the other soldiers paired off and headed to the front door of the terminal.

The Lieutenant was in discussions with the men in the truck, so Mike waited for him to finish and then asked what he should do.

"You might as well get some shut-eye in the truck. As soon as the tanks show up we can head on to the second objective, but until then we hurry up and wait and see."

Mike and the three other soldiers who weren't on patrol climbed back into the truck and tried to settle in. The driver got it started back up and headed out onto the one-way system. They drove past the McDonald's and turned onto a slipway to the right just before the road joined the M23 at the giant roundabout. This took them back to the terminal and connected back the way they'd originally come in. This time, before they reached the drop off point, they pulled into one of the first bus stops, at the very beginning of the terminal, only partially lit from the overhead lights. Here they looked to all intents and purposes like a rather specialised bus. The driver and co-driver had reclined the seats as much as they could and were trying to burrow into the upholstered padding. In the back, the seats had been folded up leaving enough room for the three other soldiers to squeeze themselves onto the floor around the central table which the Lieutenant had stood on.

Mike was a little slow in figuring out that space was limited and so stood there just in the entrance wondering where he would sleep. He was about to ask when one of the soldiers suggested he try the top cover, indicating the officer's table. He shrugged and climbed up to see what it looked like. He popped his head through the opening to peer between armoured plates which surrounded the safe end of a large machine gun. Rounds on a belt entered from the left from a square box. This was the real thing. He resolved to steer well clear of that and looked around. The gun and armoured plates rotated with him like an open-topped turret. He turned to look towards the back of the truck and could see cars as they entered the car park area.

Below him, the soldiers were already snoring. The cars eventually stopped coming down the road, and the frequency of the occasional car leaving the complex became less and less, the red brake lights the only activity outside. Mike's legs started to ache from standing on the table for so long, and he realised his mistake. The soldiers had managed to get what space there was available and now he was to all intents and purposes stuck. If he climbed down he'd be standing on the guys and the seats wouldn't fold down without hitting them, so all he could do was shuffle his weight from one leg to the other. He tried to lift himself through the hole and turned the activity into an exercise session, gently lowering himself back onto the table before locking his arms and raising his body off the table. After a rest, he decided standing was too hard and levered himself out of the hatch onto the roof of the truck. From here he could appreciate just how much additional equipment was attached to the outside. On all sides, the cattle stops were attached a few inches from the actual body of the truck. The aerials and snorkel exhaust were the obvious additions but there were also lights and cameras pointing both to the front and rear of the truck as well. He was lying on the roof, examining one of the cameras, when out of the corner of his eye he noticed the lights of cars approaching. A pair of them took the turnoff to the short-stay parking, so didn't come directly past the truck, but Mike could still see them in the distance as they parked and divulged their passengers. He couldn't be sure, but it certainly looked like they were carrying guns. AK47s if he was any judge. He jumped down and nudged one of the sleeping soldiers.

"Hey! Hey! There were some guys with guns heading towards the terminal. What do we do?"

The soldier opened his eyes, going from asleep to fully awake in an instant. Mike saw him reach for his radio and within seconds the truck was alive with motion. The back doors were opened and the four troops headed out, rifles in hand. Mike had no idea what he should do so headed after them.

They reached the door of the terminal entrance, the antiseptic white lights inside shining like the constant white glow of shopping malls and supermarkets. Ahead of them, they could hear shouts and then gunshots. A lot of gunshots in short succession overlapping each other. The other soldiers aimed their guns towards where the shouts were coming from and proceeded at a fast walk, swinging their muzzles in little arcs as they went.

Mike followed at a distance, thankful for the vest. It had made things awkward getting in and out of the hatch, and had got in the way when he had been running, but its weight put his mind at ease a little in the midst of the danger that was just beginning to filter into his realisation. He could hear running ahead and then the soldiers he was with were crouching and yelling. Ahead of them, outside a Transport for London stand, he could just make out a figure lying on the ground. Then more yelling in the background. The soldiers who he'd accompanied were now facing back the way they'd come, crouching on the spot and looking warily around.

He decided to head over to check out the result of the firefight. Judging from the looks on the men's faces, whatever had transpired was over. He walked over, thankful that the muzzles of the rifles avoided him as he approached. Ahead of him, he could see the Lieutenant and the rest of the men plus the armed policemen surrounding four figures on the ground, a widening pool of blood seeping from one of them. The AK47s were a good distance from the bodies and the police were just now finishing cuffing the three who were not bleeding. The Lieutenant broke off from talking to one of the officers as Mike approached. The officer in turn looked questioningly at Smail.

"Home Office," started Smail. The officer nodded as if that explained the attack and looked over at Mike. He felt he had to say something.

"Two cars in the drop-off zone," he managed. Then a memory of Felixstowe. "Has anyone looked at the guns?"

The cops looked at Smail who looked back and shrugged. Mike went over towards where the guns lay on the ground, one half under a seat. They certainly looked new. He bent down to smell them, but the smell of propellant was too strong for anything else to be detectable. He glanced up to see everyone watching him curiously. He got to his feet and brushed himself off. The soldiers went back to what they were doing.

"Kind of curious those guys turning up only a couple of hours after your team did, now, isn't it?" said the officer, looking suspiciously at Mike. "Anything you want to share with us? Anything else we should expect tonight? Anything the Home Office wants to tell us?"

Mike smiled wryly. "I didn't even want to be here. There's somewhere in Grinstead I need to be."

The officer looked at Smail who nodded.

"I guess we just got lucky."

Judging from the grumbling of some of the other men, they were getting hungry and Smail had just indicated to them that they should crack out the MREs, explaining in response to Mike's confused look that they were "Meals, Ready to Eat" in military parlance.

Mike had heard that military food wasn't the best, so took the opportunity to quietly suggest an alternative. "It seems to be a waste of being so close to that McDonald's, do you want me to pop over and get some food?" He didn't want to seem like he was trying to buy favour, so he grinned and added, "on the Home Office."

Smail grinned back, calling over his shoulder "Hang fire on the rat packs lads. Mr Reid here is thinking of McDonald's instead. Any objections?"

A chorus of general agreement erupted in response, the only slight dissension being Andrews, who looked disappointed as he returned the rations to the locker.

The walk across in the dark was uneventful enough, with the only traffic around being the odd taxi driver or late-night fast food junky. He was told in no uncertain terms that the sitting portion of the restaurant was shut for the night, but after explaining the size of the order the manager was a little more welcoming, especially after the payment went through. The McDonald's staff had been mopping and cleaning but sprang into action preparing the meals once given the go-ahead. Mike wondered if he would be able to claim the cost back from the Home Office before realising he was starting to believe his own mini-lie. Was it a lie if he didn't correct someone else's misconception?

The meal was too much for him to carry in one armful, so one of the staff got some oversized bags and helped him load the boxes of burgers, nuggets and fries aboard.

"What's with the army gear?" he asked.

Mike smiled wryly. "Just some exercises," he managed.

"Well, those shots earlier damn near made me shit myself. You guys should warn people when you're going to do that sort of thing."

"I'll make a note to tell the boss," Mike said then wobbled his way back to the truck with the plastic bag handles cutting into his hands and the aroma driving him to distraction. Some of the soldiers were up on the roof of the truck and as he got closer he could see them frantically gesturing to the men inside the truck. As he approached the truck with the back hatch wide open, he could overhear conversation from within.

"Yeah, but then he bent down, and get this, without a word of a lie, he sniffed the AK. Like what the fuck can you find out from what a rifle smells like? That ain't normal. And—oh hello! God that smells good, can I give you a hand?"

They distributed the food and set to.

As the conversion was replaced with the sounds of eating, Mike sought out the soldier who had been speaking as he arrived. "You make a good point about the AK," he started between mouthfuls of his burger. "We'd been told that there was a shipping container of brand new AK47s on their way into the country and I wanted to see if I could tell if it was one of them."

He thought that sharing the food and intel would surely get them onside.

"AK...47?" asked the soldier.

"Quiet, Jones. How is your burger?" broke in Smail. Mike looked around the room and, judging from the smirks and smiles, he had said something foolish. He flashed a questioning look at Smail, who leaned closer to him. "The AK47 has been discontinued for quite some time now, so unless it's been in storage for 50 years, it's probably a later model. I think those were AK15s—chambered in 5.56mm NATO calibre. The local constabulary are keeping an eye on them. They seem to think that it was a normal case and wanted witness statements. I think they must have missed their briefings."

Mike was a little annoyed by the pedantry, but tried not to show it. He wondered if his fake spy credentials were gone. Oh well, he'd been foolish to think that a round of Maccas would be enough to make bosom buddies. He was interested in what the military and police had been told though.

"What did they end up telling the police?" Mike tried.

"I'm not sure, probably what they told us. A limited insurrection, make sure that anyone you shoot is an immediate threat to life, because they're all

British."

They received notification that the tank regiment coming to relieve them had been delayed due to an engagement at their previous location, so they continued to alternately patrol the airport and then try and sleep in the truck. Mike was tempted to go over to the Hilton nearby and see if he could negotiate a rate for a room or two, but he didn't think that the news would paint the Armed Forces in a good light should that become public knowledge. Even though surely it would be better to be more fully rested from sleeping in a bed than would be possible in the back of a truck.

A very rough night later, Mike joined the men breakfasting on the All Day Breakfast ration packs, which turned out to be vaguely edible, if he was honest. The other trucks in the unit had caught up with them overnight, and so the patrols had expanded to include time on the tarmac of the airport and its perimeter. Mixing it up made the four hours on patrol a little more interesting, but only getting four hours of sleep was always going to make the next day a little hard to take—especially when every hour spent at Gatwick was another hour a Russian assassin could be looking to knock off Reggie. Eventually, a column of tanks rolled in, some of them the wide imposing tank sporting the enormous gun Mike was expecting, but also accompanied by much slimmer tanks with a collection of missiles in a small turret on top.

They waved goodbye to the tankies and climbed aboard the truck. The sky had well and truly cleared, and after they left the M23 the sun was pretty much straight ahead of them, causing moments of sunstrike. The roads were eerily empty though and, with the rain gone, the wind circulating through the truck was cool and fragrant. Their company had a number of objectives, and somewhere along the road the force split in half, three trucks setting up a road block, while Smail and Mike and the rest of the men continued on their way.

THE CHASE

They continued driving through the country towns of West Sussex. Occasionally the branches of the trees overhead would brush against the top of the truck, causing Smail to duck involuntarily. Their speed dropped as they entered a built-up area. From what Mike could see through the cab and out the front window, the streets were totally empty—not even anyone parking on the sides of the roads. And then they were back in the countryside again. This time the trees were lower and brushing against the aerials and grating more often, the roads narrower and enclosed by overgrowth. Their speed remained low and the mood in the truck changed. Mike looked from soldier to soldier. He was unable to pinpoint exactly where the change had originated, but there was a tenseness in body language and posture that matched the serious looks on their faces.

A burnt-out car on the side of the road brought the speed of the convoy down further, the back of the truck in front of them visible through the front windscreen. The driver and co-driver seemed to hum with concentration as they interrogated the surroundings, knowing full well that any blockage on the road lent itself to the perfect ambush spot. Smail was chattering on the radio, the words whipped away by the wind before Mike could make them out. He wasn't concerned because the tone wasn't excited and gave no hint of urgency.

Smail poked his head back down into the truck. "Five minutes, lads."

They pulled into a driveway, the truck in front blocking the road and the one behind already executing a three-point turn. The rear door popped open and the men departed, finding cover along the treeline or against the stone wall leading from the brick pillars holding the gate. The large black metal was off the hinges, the weight of it crushing the flowers in the garden just inside the gate. Someone had evidently driven into the gate, bending the metal and knocking the gate in, cracking the brick pillar and making it precariously off balance. A metal plaque indicated that this was indeed Eastwell Manor. That wasn't the only sign of violence—the small grass verge on the other side of the lane was a criss-cross of tyre tracks and horse hoofs and some of the smaller trees were uprooted. In each of the trucks the co-driver had taken up position on the machine gun in the hatch, and two of the three squads made their way past the broken gate along the driveway, Mike following beside Smail, trying to keep out of the way.

The men were almost perfectly silent, periodically turning and scanning the surroundings, their rifles at the ready. They followed the driveway to a car park in front of a smouldering wreck of a stately home. There were still two intact cars in the driveway, parked haphazardly a little away from the burnt-out husk. The smell was a combination of death and fire. Mike felt his stomach drop. They were too late.

The men spread out, the silence of their progress punctuated periodically by birdsong. Smail was on his radio, speaking quietly into the little microphone poking out from his helmet. All Mike could think of was what he might have done differently. Would he have been able to help Reggie if he'd come straight to the manor instead of heading to the barracks to hook up with the Scots? Or, when he'd found they'd gone to the airport instead of coming straight to Reggie, would he have been able to get a cab or an Uber? Dammit. Too many delays.

The soldiers from the first truck headed off to the left and disappeared into the woods on the boundary of the property, pausing to check out the pool house which unexpectedly stood unharmed.

The rest of them made their way through the estate nearer the burnt-out remains. They left the immediate environs, walking past what was left of a glasshouse and through an equestrian centre, the stables thankfully empty. The lane leading from the stables led back to the main road where the trucks were parked. The day had become so still by then that Mike could hear Smail radio and let the guys with machine guns on the truck know that they were coming along the road so they didn't get shot.

Smail and the section leaders discussed what they would do next.

"Our orders are to continue on to the Shoreham Power Station and secure that. We can make it there this evening. They've given us time in case we encounter opposition. So, if we can find out more about your friend, then we can follow up those leads today."

"Thanks," managed Mike.

Smail froze, staring at the ground while some piece of information was relayed via radio, before raising his eyebrows at Mike and saying, "Speaking of which..." and then addressing the men, "Patrol coming in."

Half of the men from the first truck were returning, escorting two dishevelled civilians—or maybe not civilians, as one of the soldiers was carrying an additional two guns. Not AK47s or AK15s. These looked like shotguns. There was no curved magazine and the barrel was thicker. The men had their hands zip-tied behind their backs and were wearing camouflaged hunting jackets and jeans. They were in their forties and weren't exactly in the best of shape.

"They were asleep by the fishing lake. Surrounded by beer cans and a good haul of fish in the icebox."

"Take that one to the truck, bring the other one with us," said Smail, leading the way back past the collapsed timbers of the stately home to the pool house. Mike tagged along, eager to find out what had happened to Reggie.

Smail indicated one of the sun loungers. "Can you cut him free?" and the soldier duly complied. There were four of them surrounding the man, and

Smail sent one of the soldiers away in each direction. To get away, the man would have to get past one armed soldier and then outrun the rest of the unit. "What's your name?" Smail asked the prisoner.

"I ain't telling you anything," said the man, "not until I get a lawyer."

Smail shrugged. "Fair enough," he said. There was a lengthy pause. Mike didn't say anything, trusting that Smail knew what he was doing. "It's just... see, this guy here isn't in uniform. And the reason he's not in uniform is that he works for the Home Office. But he's not here officially, you understand. Totally off the books. He's actually a... well, I want to say torturer, but the official word is interrogator, isn't it?" Smail looked over to Mike, not a trace of a smile on his face. The man looked uncertainly between Mike and Smail, trying to catch a smile or grin or any indication that this was a joke.

"Bullshit. That's against the Geneva Convention. And we don't torture. That's those others, not us."

Smail shrugged. "You're probably right. But see, I've seen this guy at work. He doesn't break a sweat. First of all, he's going to lie you on your back and zip tie you to the sun-lounger and then we'll get two of those guys over there to lift the other end of the sun-lounger so that your head is just above the water. All the blood will rush to your head. And then he'll put a towel over your head so that you can't see anything. It's funny how the other senses become more attuned when you can't see anything. Which is a pity because he's going to be pouring water over the towel. You see, your brain will be convinced that you are drowning. Drowning isn't a nice way to go— struggling for breath, fighting and thrashing. And being blind will make that feel even worse. And that's what he'll do just to get your name, let alone what he'll do if you don't tell us everything—what happened here, and where the people who used to live here are now."

By now the man's eyes were frantically searching their faces. He was slowly rubbing his wrists where the plastic zip ties had chafed.

"Oh, and those two men are just two of twenty we have in three trucks, so if you're planning on making a run for it I hope you're fitter than you look, because my men can run one and a half miles in ten minutes and I really don't think you can outrun our trucks." He let that sink in, then got to his feet. "You won't need a gag for this one; nobody is around to hear the screams. And don't worry if it goes too far. We can get more information from his friend." Smail walked off closer to the manor house and stared into the ashes.

Mike looked over at the scared man. He opened his mouth to say something. He didn't know if it was to come clean or to continue the lie, but he was saved from having to make a decision when the man stopped him.

"Fine. My name is Thomas Finlayson. What do you want to know?"

"Hi, Thomas. My name is Mike. Why don't you tell me everything, starting at the beginning? What happened here?"

Thomas eyed him warily. "It's the uprising, isn't it. We're retaking the country from the rich and corrupt."

Mike smiled agreeably and nodded. "Yes, I understand that, but I mean what happened specifically here? Who burnt the house?"

"Ah," Thomas replied, the penny dropping. "That was the team based in Grinstead. They did the Earl's place then they came here. After that, they went onto the next one. Me and Fred were the caretaker team—we make sure none of the rich folk come back or anyone loots the house."

"No one loots the burnt down house?"

"Yeah, anyway we got a little bored so we got hold of some beers and Fred had some fishing poles in his car, so we settled in. None of the rich folk came back so we spent more and more time at the fishing lake. We were supposed to relieve the day shift but when we came back last night they had already gone, so we settled in for a good night."

"Tell me more about the Grinstead team. How many of them were

132

there?"

"I don't know—three cars. Maybe ten? Twelve?"

"Good, did you recognise any of them? Did you know their names?"

"No, we arrived as they were lighting the place up."

"And what happened to the people who were living here?"

"They were about to line them up and shoot them, but one of the guys in the team knew them or something and said that they should take them back to the re-education camps. Said that they weren't ancestral money."

"This is really important Thomas. Where are those re-education camps?"

Thomas' face dropped. "I...I don't know. I mean, I was told, but I didn't pay attention. Uh, maybe Fred knows. They set them up in schools—one for men and one for women. You're not going to torture me, are you? I would tell you if I knew—I'm not a bad man, I just got swayed by the crowd."

Mike stared at him for a few minutes until his ramblings died away, then stood up. "Stay here," he said as he strode away towards the truck where they'd taken Fred. Smail joined him as he passed the house.

"Did you get what you needed?"

"Almost—he was taken to a 're-education camp'. I'm hoping our friend Fred here will be able to tell me exactly where that is."

Smail nodded.

They approached the back of the truck where Fred was being held and Smail sent the soldiers guarding him away. The co-driver who was manning the machine gun was sent away with the driver to brew up a cup of tea. Fred was sitting in one of the seats along the wall of the truck.

Fred looked at Smail and Mike impassively. Mike waited for Smail to launch into some blood-chilling introduction as he had done with Thomas. Instead, Smail casually sat in one of the seats opposite Fred and leant back, totally at ease. "Fred, isn't it? Your friend Thomas was most forthcoming. We don't actually need anything from you. So we're almost ready to let you two go back to what you were doing. We just need a couple of points confirmed."

Fred blinked, surprised. But he seemed happy enough at how things seemed to be panning out. "Sure, if Tom has already told you, I guess it wouldn't hurt."

Smail smiled encouragingly. "So he told us the re-education camp was at the Queen Victoria Hospital—we passed that on the way in."

Fred frowned. "No, the women's one is at Mapham Park and the men's at Thistledown Park."

Smail frowned, puzzled. "I don't understand."

"The golf courses. The symbol of the elite. The perfect place to re-educate. Jeez, Tom never did pay attention. The Hospital?"

Smail smiled his thanks. "Fred, do you have any ID on you? I just have to write up this conversation, and then you can go."

Fred's smile faded. "The orders we got were not to have any identifying documentation on us. No wallet. No driving license, no passport, no nothing."

Smail nodded. "Makes sense. Do you have your phone?" he held out his hand.

"There's no signal, we checked."

Smail took a notepad and a golf pencil out of an inside pocket from his camouflage jacket and wrote a little receipt. "Let's see, it's an iPhone 7. What's your phone number?" That was written on the receipt as well. Smail rummaged around in a courier's bag on the floor of the truck, re-emerging with a thumb-sized white sticker which he applied to the back of the phone. On this, he wrote the phone number and what seemed a random assortment of numbers and letters. "You can apply to get this back from Her Majesty's government—probably in a week. The details will be published in newspapers. If you give me your email address we'll send out the details directly."

"Hey, you can't do that —that's my property. You can't just steal that. There are laws."

Smail waited for the diatribe to die down. "Things like that have been... suspended... while we sort this situation out."

A thought occurred to Mike. "Are the cars unlocked?"

Fred nodded absently, more focused on the loss of his phone.

Mike slipped out of the truck, Smail following him. Smail sent one of the soldiers into the truck to keep an eye on Fred, and he and Mike approached the two cars which were parked none too neatly in front of the house. As he suspected, the glove boxes revealed receipts and service records of the car, which in turn revealed the full names and addresses of the two men.

"So, any chance of a lift to Thistledown Park Golf Course?"

135

THE GOLF COURSE

While it wasn't on the way to the power station, Smail thought that they would be able to take a slight detour to check out the Golf Course. He sent the other two trucks ahead to secure the M23 just outside Crawley—an important junction on the road from Brighton to London and an important approach to Gatwick Airport. Mike thought that Smail was more than a little intrigued by the side quest nature of his requests. The hunt for one man in a nation of 65 million did have a certain 'Saving Private Ryan' feel to it. Smail had made meticulous notes in his notebook about the phone and its owner before returning the phone and then releasing Fred and Tom. Now, the convoy of three trucks headed slowly down the main country roads towards their destination, the sun coming through the canopy and birds keeping up a steady chorus. The trees met above their heads, and the road seemed to be driving through a tunnel of overgrowth, with only sporadic glimpses of the sky above.

It was only a ten-minute drive, so in no time at all they'd turned off the main road and entered a clearing beside a large country house. The road continued on but, from Mike's vantage point, he could see Smail's legs rotate to keep the house in line with the muzzle of the machine gun on the roof. They weren't harassed from the house though and made their way a few hundred metres further down the lane. On one side of it, a few spindly trees separated the lane from a collection of farming buildings. On the other side, the forest was a little denser and came right up to the side of the lane. Ahead of them, the lane passed through a gate that led to the golf course. The rustic wooded surrounds then gave way to the immaculately maintained lawns of the golf course. They parked in the vacant parking lot in front of a three-car garage, the roller doors pulled closed. The soldiers exited the truck and made their way up to the clubrooms. Their parking spot was secluded out of sight of the clubrooms and so they were able to make their way to the front doors before being seen.

The unpreparedness of the guards inside was so absolute that two of the men walked in and were at the interior doors before the guards realised that they weren't part of the insurrection. The guard had left his gun leaning against the wall and was leaning lazily and dangerously in an office chair behind the counter. Andrews held a finger to his lips as one of the other men zip-tied his hands behind him and took him back out to the truck. The only sound was a slight grunt as the zip tie tightened. The other guard at least had his gun on him, but was facing into the restaurant. He was disabled pretty quickly by Andrews and left for one of the others to zip tie. By then, Mike and Smail had made their way fully into the building and had a clear view of the could situation.

The restaurant had been turned over as some sort of open prison. About twenty people sat with their backs against the wall while the furniture was stacked in a makeshift wall in the centre of the space. Some of the men inside showed signs of having been in a fight, with one of them bleeding badly from his nose, his shirt covered in an upside-down V of blood. When the guards were disabled, there was a general clamour and demands to be released. Smail held his hands up for silence. As the demands receded, he finally made his speech.

"Gentlemen, your attention, please. We need to take your details and a brief account of the last few days, but before we get started on that, this gentleman is looking for someone." He beckoned for Mike to come forward.

"Reggie Rutherford," Mike called out. "Is there a Reggie Rutherford here? Or does anyone know Reggie?"

In the background, a tall older gentleman stood up with a hand hesitatingly held up. "I'm Reggie," he managed. He seemed no worse for wear from his misadventures, looking a little grubby with dirt and ash marks on his clothes, but no blood or sign of injury.

"I'm Mike Reid," he said as Reggie broke away from the other former prisoners.

"Oh hi! How was the apartment?" Reggie asked, shaking his hand heartily.

Mike couldn't help but smile at the total disregard for the current circumstances. "The apartment was fine, Reg. Really good. But I'm afraid the Manor has seen better days."

"Have you found Meredith? Marcus and Zoe?" Reg asked, placing both hands on Mike's shoulders and peering into his eyes with ferocity.

Mike was surprised by the switch in intensity. "Not yet," he said, not knowing who those other people were, but guessing Meredith was his wife. He was a bit at a loss on how to explain his presence. "I had to tell you that you might be in danger," he managed. Then when he realised how ridiculous it sounded, he tried again. "I've been looking for you for a few days now. I got a bit waylaid by these good folks... divergent responsibilities... you understand, I'm sure. But tell me what happened."

Reggie cocked his head and made a point of thinking for a second, before beckoning for Mike to follow him. He walked to the restaurant kitchen and started going through the industrial fridge there, exiting with a full tray of eggs. "We've had nothing but crisps the whole time we've been here. I figure to make the world's biggest omelette. We can talk while I cook it. Is there any cheese in there?"

Mike managed to piece together a view of what had happened with only occasional prompting and clarifications required. Apparently, Reg had seen and smelled the fire at the neighbouring house and gone to see if he could help. He'd witnessed those responsible for setting the fire shoot the Earl and had sent his nephew and niece to a bunker they had near their cottage. Then he'd returned to the Manor and attempted to escape with his wife. The team who had attacked and burned the Earl's house then arrived and captured him and Meredith. The houseguest, groundsman and housekeeper had all gotten away. The death squad were going to line him and his wife up against the wall and shoot them but one of the squad had been a worker on one of Reg's businesses, and had spoken out on their behalf. Apparently the fact that he was new money and not old was somehow enough to get a stay of execution. He'd been taken here and spent two sleepless nights watching other men being brought in. The guards had been instructed to stop them from talking to each other, but as the prisoner numbers increased, the guards were soon outnumbered and started to be concerned about being overwhelmed. That explained the ease with which they'd been able to waltz in and liberate the place, thought Mike.

"Your lot would want some eggs too, yeah?" asked Reggie, surveying the pile of sticky yellow mess he'd made. There was about a fifty/fifty mix of cheese to eggs. A pair of kilo blocks were sliced and added to the eggs as they cooked. As the two of them assembled a pile of plates and started to serve it up, the aroma attracted the prisoners and they started to filter into the kitchen one by one. "I think I saw a loaf of bread in the fridge and there was definitely some butter in there, so grab a plate." The prisoners cycled through the kitchen, one asking if there was anything to drink. The bar had shutters covering it with a padlock through the clasp. The shutters covered the narrower side of the bar too, so nobody could get behind it either. They had to settle for pint glasses full of tap water. One of the prisoners came up to their ad hoc serving station and, in all seriousness, asked if they had anything vegan. Mike and Reggie looked at each other. Incredulously, Mike turned back and told the prisoner to have a look in the fridge.

As the man with all the blood on his shirt came through and collected a plate, Mike heard Reggie thank him in a low voice. As he shuffled off and the soldiers started coming through, Mike and Reggie were relieved of their serving duties and found a corner of the restaurant to sit and eat. 'What was that about?" asked Mike.

"So last night a guy came through on a motorbike. He pulled up and came in and was asking about Eastwell Manor. The guards didn't know where each of us had come from so they just gestured at random, and the guy thought that they were pointing out that guy in particular. So he came over and popped the guy. Boom, down he goes, bleeding everywhere. Our bikie gets out some papers and compares the guy on the floor with the paper and decides he wasn't it, and then goes person to person through the room, comparing them to some photos in the papers. I guess no one looked enough like the guy in the papers, so out he goes on his bike."

"Was he Russian? The biker guy? Did he speak in a Russian accent?"

A mischievous light danced across Reggie's eyes. "Yes and no," he said.

"What do you mean yes and no?"

"So he didn't have an accent. English sounding anyway."

"So, no then? Not Russian?"

"Mmmm, not really. He may not have sounded Russian, but the writing on the papers he had was acrylic."

"You mean Cyrillic?"

"Oh yeah, that. You know, backwards Ns and backwards Rs, that sort of thing."

Mike was quiet for a while, thinking. Reggie munched away happily on his eggs. "Would you recognise him if you saw him again?" asked Mike eventually.

"Oh, absolutely!" answered Reggie, obviously feeling more alive with a full belly. "Now, about Meredith and the kids?"

Mike was a little on the back foot. "Uh... we understand that your wife has been taken to the women's re-education camp at Mapham Park, but there was no mention of any children being taken from Eastwell Manor.

Where did you say they had gone?"

Conflicting emotions rolled across Reggie's face. "The kids went to a bunker on the property and I think it's good news that nobody has mentioned them. I tried to tell them where the entrance was but it's a secret bunker so it's quite hard to find. But Meredith—can you take me to Mapham Park?"

Mike was a bit lost now that he had found Reggie. It had been his mission for so many days and now that he had repaid the debt it seemed that there were still loose ends to be tied up. "Wait here," he told Reggie and got up to find Smail.

"Smail, I have some intelligence I need to talk with the Home Office about. Can you secure me a line with a guy named Grayson?"

"I'll see if I can get through to them but, just so you know, we'll have to head out soon if we're to secure the power station before nightfall."

"OK, let me know how you get on. Did you manage to get some eggs?"

A big smile lit up Smail's face. "They were just what the doctor ordered, thanks."

A little while later Mike was called over to the truck and headed down. The soldiers were still taking statements, writing out longhand the sometimes rambling and incoherent stream of memories of the previous few days from the prisoners. Only two of the soldiers were so employed, the others either patrolling nearby or loitering from vantage points upstairs.

A large radio was in the truck and the co-driver handed it over, telling him it was Grayson.

"Hello, Grayson? It's Mike."

"Good to hear from you, Mike. I understand you gave a good account of yourself at Gatwick. Well done."

Mike frowned. "I'm not sure I actually helped there but thanks anyway.

Listen, I tracked down your agent in Grinstead."

Grayson was quiet before responding. "Uh... no you didn't. I'm not sure who you've found there, but we rounded up the last of the ten two days ago. Eyewitness matches and everything. Who have you found there?"

Now it was Mike's turn to pause. "Uh... my friend in Grinstead mentioned a Russian who seemed to be on a mission like the one you told me about. He was looking for someone from Eastwell Manor, and while my friend was from Eastwell Manor, he wasn't the guy that the Russian was looking for. Are you sure all the ten are accounted for?"

Grayson was quick to respond to that. "Absolutely. I used your checklist and we had multiple people confirm their identities. They're all being debriefed as we speak, so yes I'm sure that they're accounted for. Can you tell me more about your Russian?"

Mike recounted what Reggie had said about the Russian, and detected an uptick in interest when he mentioned the Russian's motorbike. "I see. Listen carefully, Mike. It seems you've stumbled across The Handler—the man who was feeding instructions to Svetlana. We found some circumstantial evidence that suggested that he rode a motorbike and, while it's tenuous, it's too much of a coincidence to ignore. It's quite important that we talk to this fellow as there are some legacy operations that we have tied to him which predate the current events. We think he might have been one of those who precipitated the current environment, so I can't stress how much we're interested in having a little chat with him. Did anyone else have any interactions with him apart from your friend? Does anyone know where he went?"

"Smail and his team are debriefing the other prisoners now, I can check with them before they're released. But Smail needs to head to the power station soon, so I'm going to be without a ride. If we do find a clue, we might need you to swing a change in their orders, otherwise I'll be chasing the Russian on his motorcycle in a golf cart."

THE MAN IN THE HOTEL CEILING

"Very droll. I'll see what I can do. Thanks, Mike."

Mike handed the radio handset back to the driver with both hands and headed back up to the clubhouse.

Smail was supervising the debriefings and, by the looks of things, they weren't going very well. Mike could almost see the steam coming out of Smail's ears as he tried to keep his cool. "So you're saying that they took your Rolex, but that you couldn't describe the man who took it? That's understandable, sir, it was at night. But I'm afraid your claim will be on your insurance company, not the government."

The man opposite him sitting on a restaurant chair frowned in confusion. "Well, why are we talking about it then?"

Smail took a couple of deep breaths. "As I said at the beginning, we're collecting witness statements to try and establish who did what, when and to whom. The statements will form the basis for the prosecution of those who committed crimes. It's not an itemised list of everything that you've lost or had stolen. Let's take five—grab a drink from the bar."

Mike looked over and the bar had been opened. Maybe someone found a key, though Mike suspected that brute force may have been involved. Smail had seen Mike approach and they headed through the huge glass doors to the patio overlooking the first hole. The sun was shining, the birds were chirping and the slight breeze just took the edge off the heat. The surroundings were still impeccable, although the grass would need a mow soon, the recent gorgeous recent weather having encouraged new growth. They sat at one of the tables and Smail sighed, letting the tension leave him before turning to Mike. "So, what did you learn?"

"Slight change to my mission," started Mike. "There is a man on a motorbike here last night and we need to track him down. I'll need to talk to all the prisoners to see if anyone saw or heard anything that might be a clue as to where he went."

"I don't fancy your chances. As a rule, they're not the most observant lot.

I'm just waiting for one of them to claim that he had a couple of Rembrandts in the car that was stolen and that we'll have to reimburse them."

"So why are you asking them all those questions?"

Smail sighed and rubbed his face. "Think about it like this: we either have the worst case of civil disobedience in the nation's history, or else we have the most one-sided civil war we've ever seen. Either way, we're going to end up with a very large proportion of the country implicit in crimes ranging from Tom and Fred who are guilty of poaching in the lake and drinking beer while possessing a firearm, all the way to those death squads doing the executions. Now, ask yourself, when things go back to normal, how are we going to punish everyone who needs punishing? We can't put everyone in jail, can we? We don't have enough jails. And none of the cases will stand up in court—there's no evidence, and no way to discover good enough evidence because that would mean investigating them for the next decade. So we'll have to focus our efforts on those committing capital crimes. And the others that we can prove, we'll give them a slap on the wrist, say 'naughty' and give them a suspended sentence. If you do anything else we'll give you both barrels, but keep your nose clean and we'll turn a blind eye to your little demeanours. But those guys in the cars going house to house with their guns? Those guys we need to get. So we take witness statements. And if they might be able to recognise the faces we put a little asterisk for the police to follow up when they can. And if we can get times then we can get a bit of a timeline of what happened when. And if we can get enough corroborating evidence we might be able to hold people to account for what they did."

"That sounds great, and then we can get back to normal, right?"

Smail was quiet for a while. "Normal might be a little way away." He held up four fingers. "Four groups. Group One and Two. They were hands-on involved with the insurrection. They believed in the cause. Enough to act. They are guilty. Group One did the really bad stuff. So they're either going to be locked up or looking over their shoulder for a long time. Group Two didn't, so they're going to be defensive. 'I didn't kill anyone—get those guys, not me.' Group three are the great majority. They might have some sympathy for the insurrection, which will make them feel guilty. Even if they didn't support the insurrection they will feel like they have to distance themselves from the cause, in case they get lumped in with them. Then you have the victims. Those that survived will want those who did the crimes to pay."

"OK"

"So group one. Guilty. Group two. Guilty and defensive. Group three. Guilty and reactionary. Group four. Vengeful. Tell me, Mike, what's the next year going to be like? Take your man Reggie there. He was spared because someone knew he was new money, not old. What is Christmas going to be like on his estate? What's the village fete going to be like? The new Earl wondering which of the people buying homemade jams killed his cousin. The people who looted and burned trying to avoid people's eyes. Those that stayed at home hiding under the table, scared of talking about it in case they get accused of being involved. Because everybody's alibi is the same. 'I stayed at home. Nobody saw me except the wife and kids.'"

Mike nodded slowly. "I guess that makes it even more important that we find the ringleaders and make sure that they really pay."

Smail nodded in agreement.

THE FINAL CLUE

Twenty men recalling what happened over the last three or four days had driven Smail to distraction. But Mike was able to zoom in on the last night alone, and that made all the difference. At first, the men who had already given their statements to Smail were reluctant to talk to him but, when they found out that they would not be reliving the traumatic event of the night of the fires and gunshots, he got a lot more cooperation. As usual in such situations, there was a core set of facts that everyone agreed on, a set of facts that had a range of agreement, and things that all but one agreed on.

There was widespread agreement on the height (average) and build (normal) of The Handler. He had a sweep of dark hair on top, and no facial hair. He wore black leathers and had a helmet. He spoke English and, when pressed, nobody said they had detected an accent.

Some claimed to have noticed a particular element of the leathers, the boots, the helmet. But someone else would have noticed the same element, the details of which would be different.

Apparently, The Handler had arrived, walked in and spoken to the guard. Punched the man with the blood on his shirt. Made them all line up, and checked each prisoner against a photo. Then walked out again.

Going through the notes, Mike switched to investigator mode. The man had arrived, done something and then left. Normally he'd look for video footage—the bar! Did it have any cameras? He got up and ran into the restaurant. There they were, on the ceiling, one above the bar looking at the register. The other two in the restaurant. He dashed out to the foyer. Sure enough—one there. Out the front—another one, looking across the car park. The general agreement was that he'd arrived from the back, the same way as Mike and the soldiers had arrived, but there weren't any cameras looking that way at all. Only four cameras?

He went back to the bar and looked for a door marked "Office". Nothing with a sign specifically saying 'office' on it, but there was a door marked "Private" which seemed promising. It was locked, but thinking about the bar had been opened up, which gave him hope for a key. So he sought out Smail, who was just returning from the direction of the truck.

"Smail, how did you get the bar open? Is there a key? I have a door I need to open."

Smail laughed and went over to the bar and held up a crowbar. "Opens all sorts of padlocks, and it might be good enough to get through this door of yours too."

Mike showed him the door and, with a little bit of effort, they managed to jimmy the door open, wrecking the door jam and chipping the door itself quite badly. The office beyond was like every other office Mike had seen. Folders on shelves, a desk with papers flowing from inbox to outbox, Post-it notes stuck to a monitor. Calendar on the desk with various holidays and tax dates asterisked, and a computer tucked underneath the desk. A black box sat on a shelf, the nexus of a collection of wires which disappeared through holes in the ceiling. A single cable connected it to the computer. Smail was beside him and smirked as Mike turned on the computer.

"Do you think you will be able to guess the password?" he asked as the prompt came up on the screen.

"I won't have to," responded Mike. "Nine times out of ten there's a Post-it with the password on it attached to the screen." And there it was. It was a strong password—lots of special characters and numbers. But the security was entirely undone by having it in writing beside the machine.

A few minutes later, he was in.

"Can you read out the brand name on that black box there, please?" he asked Smail.

A quick search later and he had the program running which interfaced with the digital video system. He pulled up the list of available dates, confirmed the date and rough time that everyone agreed The Handler had been in the restaurant and scrolled through to that time.

They had coverage of him approaching the front desk but, because he'd come through from the back, there weren't any shots of him front on. Nevertheless, there was enough to confirm that he was of average height, with a stocky build and a sweep of black hair, and was wearing black motorbike leathers. No sign of a helmet though.

The remaining footage was from the restaurant itself and, because they'd effectively shoved all the tables and chairs into the middle of the room and placed all the prisoners in the corner, there wasn't any footage of the interrogation or assault. At a time that fitted what they'd been told, there was a fleeting glimpse of the man leaving, but moving too fast and at bad angles so that nothing more could really be gleaned about his appearance. There was nothing in his hands apart from a thin manila folder with a couple of pieces of paper partially sticking out. No writing discernible via the video. Mike was starting to get that tickle in the back of the brain he usually got just before making a realisation that broke the back of an investigation.

The thing that Mike had learnt over the years of investigation was that video doesn't lie. Data don't lie. If a swipe card had been used to get into a building and left a data trail, you could trust the data. To a point. He'd had someone change the date and time on a computer because the suspect had figured out that it was the computer that was used for the logging of the door access. They could then come and go and the system would provide an alibi for the lawbreaking which was happening on a different site at a later time. The investigation team had been lucky there—the only way they'd caught onto the lie was that someone had uncharacteristically turned up to catch up on some work over the weekend, before the suspect had returned the computer to the correct date and time. It had taken a single interview to establish the actual time of entry of the weekend worker, calculate the difference and then see how the circumstances had changed. A piece or two of corroborating evidence blew the alibi out of the window. Mike had been particularly proud of that one, even if he'd just been very lucky.

People, on the other hand, were fallible. Data may not be infallible but it was definitely consistent. Mike addressed the room, thanking them for their help so far in both their full written testimony as well as the subsequent questions. He just had a couple of additional questions, if they would be so kind. There were a few grumbles, but Mike felt pretty sure that it was just lowkey dissatisfaction.

There were three follow-up questions. When the man came in, did he put the helmet on the front desk, or did he have it in his hand when he looked at everybody's faces? Did you hear the motorbike pull up on the gravel out the front in the car park, or on the flat concrete out the back near the first hole? And, lastly, did the motorbike have a low chug-chug-chug sound like a Harley, or more of an electric whine like a four-stroke?

After giving them the questions and some time to think about their answers, Mike got them alone to see what each of them thought. Half of the ex-prisoners were adamant that the man had put his helmet on the desk at the front desk. And that he'd arrived at the back door. There was less certainty as to the sound the engine made. Some said that they didn't know, some that there was no sound at all, and others were pretty equally split. Mike was close to having his privately-held and unshared hypothesis confirmed to his own satisfaction, when he came to Reggie.

"Hey, Reggie, just some really simple questions for you. Sorry I didn't ask them before. But, if you can, cast your mind back to the night of the man in the leathers for me. Close your eyes if it helps. So question one: Did the man put his helmet on the desk in the foyer or did he have it in his hand when he checked faces?"

Reggie took him seriously and closed his eyes, replaying the night's events.

"I couldn't see the front desk from the restaurant where we were being held, and I don't think anyone else could either. I know that the man didn't have it in the room because he had that folder with the paper. The one with the Cyrillic writing."

Mike was impressed. Most people's brains fill in the blanks of partial stories. Completing stories with only partial information was an important ability, but knowing when the brain did it and when you actually knew all the facets of the story usually took a considerable amount of self-awareness.

"Awesome, thanks for that. Now did you hear the motorbike pull up out front on the gravel driveway, or out the back on the concrete?"

"I didn't hear a motorbike pull up or drive off."

"Ah, OK. So, if you didn't hear him pull up or drive off, then you can't think of what the engine might have sounded like? Like a low down chug-chug sound or a higher pitched whine?"

"Nope, one minute he wasn't there, and then he was there, and then he disappeared after he'd checked all the faces. Man, he was in a foul mood. I'll never forget the look on his face."

"Cheers, Reggie. I might need you to ID the guy if we find him. Would that be OK?"

"Sure, but can I use your cell phone? They took mine and I really need to call Meredith and tell her that I'm OK. And the kids must be petrified."

"As soon as that's possible we'll get you in touch with them all but we think the guy we're after is the one behind all this, so it's important that we bring him to justice."

"I understand all that, but you don't know Meredith. Or my sister. Oh, man, nothing had better have happened to the kids."

"I'll do what I can, Reg. I've got some more questions to ask—don't go too far, OK?"

"Sure, will do, Mike."

The other responses to the questions followed the same pattern as the non-Reggie answers. Mike wondered if all new money men had an issue with saying that they didn't know. Or maybe they had generated their wealth from being able to see patterns where others didn't. Either way, they were consistent with their answers—no helmet in hand, no sound of approach and total inconsistency with the sound of the engine.

He called Smail over. "You got a second?"

Smail came over. "Hey, I got some new orders. I'm to give you every assistance in your mission, but still make it to the power station by nightfall."

Mike was flummoxed. "How are you supposed to do that?"

"I'll show initiative," replied Smail deadpan. "So how can I help you?"

"We might need to collect your men for an assault," he said and then paused, letting that sink in. "The house we went past on the way in? I think that's the headquarters for this section of the operation."

Smail was all attention now. "Why do you think that?"

Mike shrugged. "This guy is supposed to be the ringleader. He turns up and nobody hears a motorbike or sees his helmet. Yet he's in leathers. And nobody heard any tires crunching on the gravel out the back where we parked. Even if he'd been in a golf cart, they would have heard him pull up. So he walked. And unless he's got some radio gear in a tree beside a bunker on the par-three fourth hole, I figure he's in the comfort of that house, rather than the farmhouses alongside the track. What do you think?"

Smail weighed it up in his mind. "Sounds like we're going to be having a bit of fun before our sprint to Brighton."

He assembled the men and, while Mike's money was on the main house, they knew they would have to clear the farm buildings first. There was too much opportunity for anyone in those buildings to see the soldiers passing by then pop up behind them and mow them down. Smail briefed the men at the truck and then they were away, the soldiers in two lines behind the truck, the co-driver manning the machine gun and Mike firmly tucked into the seat inside the truck. He'd asked Smail whether bullets would get through the truck walls and was told that the armour was designed for protection against the original AK47 and that the modern version was of a lower calibre than that, so he should be fine. A little TV screen beside the inside of the exit door at the rear of the truck showed the view immediately outside the doors, and Mike could see the fronts of the two first men in the lines behind.

Mike smiled at the crunch of the gravel under the tyres of the truck. It seemed to be confirmation of his logic about the motorcycle earlier. The truck slowly made its way up the incline to the gate where the track and the treeline began. A slight pause and then they turned off the track and along a small side driveway to the courtyard which ran parallel to the track they'd just left that joined the road to the golf course. The courtyard was bordered by low-slung farming buildings and, from the outside, Mike hadn't been able to see if they held bales of hay or tractors or something more dangerous. As they pulled into the courtyard, the interiors of the sheds became visible and their caution proved to be excessive. Most of the sheds were practically empty—an odd trailer sitting forlornly in one corner and an old rusting tractor attached to some sort of wide mowing device in another, but nothing else of note. There was a driveway which led up to the house they'd passed, running parallel to the lane that they had come down earlier that day, which exited the courtyard ahead of them, following the rise of the gentle incline.

The house had just appeared behind the surrounding trees and through the front windscreen Mike could make out the details. It was two storeys with maybe a third floor in the roof attic space. It was clad in the pale off-white sandstone that was common in this part of England, with white sash

152

windows and a dusty red-tiled roof. That's all that Mike saw before flashes from the top windows were matched by a calm voice from the gunner "Contact right, suppressing," and the deafening sound of the machine gun from the roof. The odd plink, plink reverberated through the passenger section as the incoming rounds ricocheted off the outside of the truck's armour. The truck continued its steady progress forward and, very soon after that, the firing stopped in both directions. By that time the truck was a stone's throw from the building and the soldiers who had been following in the shelter of the truck disappeared from the screen above the door and reappeared in the front windscreen then made their way into the building.

The machine gunner kept his gun trained on the windows above, rotating the turret to left and right. After the deafening roar of the machine gun, the silence was unnatural and complete. Mike was becoming concerned about the length of time that the men had been away when he heard the driver talk on the radio, half-turn and tell him that he could go inside now.

He unbelted himself and opened the rear door, letting himself out into the afternoon sun. As he turned towards the house, he started to appreciate the impact of the machine gun on the brief firefight that had just occurred. The windows had totally disappeared, and the walls around them bore the marks of the suppressive fire. He made his way to the front door of the house and called out before heading inside. He trusted the soldiers not to shoot him, but... best to be sure, right?

Smail answered his call "Up here."

The interior of the house was very fine—lots of polished marble and gilt decoration. Mike headed up a suitably impressive staircase, a skylight illuminating the stairwell, the effect somewhat ruined by bullet holes on the walls on the first-floor landing, making a ruin of the family photographs and serious-looking men in hunting tweeds standing at attention alongside King Charles spaniels. The soldiers were in a room that overlooked the entrance to the house. As he entered, Mike saw that it was covered in broken glass and smashed masonry. Two bodies had been covered in rugs.

The room smelled of burning—not the earthy tones of a fire keeping the winter chills at bay—but the smell of burnt paper. As he entered, Smail was crouching near the fireplace, fishing out small sections of paper from the mass of ashes and embers. A man in a T-shirt and jeans had his arms zip-tied behind his back and was lying uncomfortably on his stomach on the polished wooden floorboards. Andrews stood behind him with his gun held casually but the muzzle never far from the back of the man's head. Mike didn't know what had happened, but it didn't seem like the room liked this new fellow.

"Two dead in the front room, a couple in the backyard—presumably the former owners. Dead execution style and this guy was shovelling papers into the fire like his life depended on it. Needed a bit of persuading to stop. No sign of our friend in the leathers."

Mike crouched beside Smail in front of the fire. "Anything left at all?"

"Nothing in the fire."

"They've arranged for a boat owner at Newhaven Marina to ferry people 'fleeing the Terror' over to France. He leaves every day at midday to avoid suspicion. If the uprising got into trouble they would be able to escape disguised as refugees. If we're lucky then our friend The Handler won't have made today's sailing and will be waiting for the next one first thing tomorrow morning. But all this doesn't alter our mission—we have to go to Shoreham now."

"Did you tell your superiors about the Russian? About the headquarters? About the boat?"

"They'll pass that on to the Home Office in good time I would imagine, but our orders are very clear—we have to go to Shoreham. A fully operating power grid is essential for when things get back to normal and Shoreham is a vital component of that."

Mike could tell that Smail would rather hunt down the ringleader but, to his credit, he was at least parroting the official line.

"Is there any way we can intercept the boat? Coastguard, navy, helicopters?"

"Like I said, I can pass the information up the chain of command and hope that they take action but don't forget we're operating on a lot of assumptions. There may not be enough justification to move resources from where they're needed to follow up on a slim chance of catching this guy. And we don't know what resources are available either."

"Well, tell you what, can you maybe give me a lift as far as you're going and give me a gun?"

Smail didn't say anything for a while. When he finally looked up at Mike, he had a sadness in his eyes.

"Mike, I can't give you a gun. We're accountable for all our firearms, and that's as it should be. I can't and I wouldn't, even if I could. Do you know how to use a gun? Have you had any training? It's not like the movies, you know."

Mike tried not to pout. "Well, how hard can it be?"

Smail smiled briefly. "Our lads train hard to make it look that effortless. A lot of training."

Mike nodded, understanding. "And it's insulting for me to suggest that I could just pick one up and use it, right? It doesn't have to be one of those rifles—it could just be a pistol. They're easier aren't they?"

A look of annoyance flashed across Smail's face. "Smaller. Lighter. Less likely to kill the person behind your target. But no, I can't let you have my sidearm. And I very strongly advise against picking up one of those AKs. Look, you're not a soldier, you don't look like a soldier and you don't act like a soldier. If you take a weapon, any weapon, and someone sees you, it'll be obvious that you're not on the side of Her Majesty's Armed Forces and if you're not on our side, then you must be the enemy. And you will end up in jail, despite any claims of working for the Home Office. Or worse. You could end up like those two in there." The sad look returned. "What's going on? You have all the demeanour of a man taking this personally. Let it go. If they can get boots on the ground at Newhaven, then they'll need you to ID the guy. And if they don't get there in time, there's nothing you can do. It's just too dangerous for civilians. This is a war."

Mike paused. Then in a rush he described how the Russians had killed the perfectly innocent Gary, causing his possibly demented husband to spend time living in a ceiling crawlspace. He reined himself in as the lack of sleep combined with the sadness of Gary and Gavin's story plus the overwhelming feeling of futility and helplessness brought him increasingly close to tears. He took a deep breath.

"I understand what you're saying about guns. And if this is where our paths split, I wish you and your men every success. Where are you taking our friend there?"

Smail was just as glad as Mike for the change of subject. "We've been instructed to take him to Quebec Barracks in Brighton. That's another reason we can't take you—full truck."

"Are you going now?"

"We're burning daylight."

"What will happen to the ex-prisoners?"

"They're free to go, can you let them know?"

"Sure." Mike walked down the stairs with Smail and Andrews brought the prisoner down behind them. Mike stood in the doorway as they loaded the soldiers and prisoner into the back of the truck and the co-driver took his place in the front cab. As he passed he gave Mike a nod and thanked him for the McDonald's. Mike watched the truck drive up the driveway, and then stalked back inside.

NEWHAVEN

Mike sat at the table in the dining room. Through one set of windows he could see a triple garage and driveway leading out onto the main road. Another set of windows looked out onto the back of the building. Pristine lawns surrounded a huge swimming pool, edged by mature trees and hedges. The afternoon sun was shining, the birds were tweeting sweetly but all Mike could think about was the chaos and death, the two bodies of the owners behind the garage, and the two upstairs, and how the man responsible, or at least partly responsible, seemed to be going to get away without being punished for his crimes. In Mike's profession, you did the job because you loved catching the bad guys, or because it was an intellectual exercise in solving complex problems. A visceral desire to hurt someone didn't tend to come into it. He wasn't sure he liked this feeling, but the fire of purpose was strangely comforting.

Back to basics. What did he want? To bring The Handler to justice. Whatever that meant. What did he know? Presumably, where The Handler was going and where he would be tomorrow at noon. Unless the boatman was convinced to take him straight away. But he didn't know what The Handler looked like. He would only have to take his leathers off and have a haircut and he would be anonymous. So he needed to get to Newhaven as soon as possible to stop him from escaping the country. And he needed to take Reg because he was the only one who knew what the guy looked like.

To do that, he needed to find wheels. He looked around the kitchen for a key hook and wasn't surprised to find a selection of keys in a bowl on the breakfast bench between kitchen and dining room. He grabbed all of them and headed towards the garage. He examined the three cars there, one in particular catching his eye. That would do very nicely indeed, he thought, as he clicked the garage door opener and unlocked the door to a very expensive car.

He pulled up to the golf club rooms in a spray of gravel, leapt out and bounded up the stairs to the back entrance. The ex-prisoners' faces popped up at the restaurant windows like meerkats and any lingering fear from having heard the firefight at the house melted as they recognised him from earlier. He held up his hands for quiet and, as the hubbub died down, he sought out Reg and nodded towards the door.

"Hi, everyone. Lieutenant Smail had to go, so he sent me to thank you for your statements and to say that you're all free to leave. Reg and I have a boat to catch." And with that he headed for the door, collaring Reg as he went by and ignoring the shouted questions that followed him out of the door. He told Reg to get in the car, waiting just long enough for the door to close before giving the car a little too much gas and flooring it up the driveway, past the house and onto the main roads.

"Where are we going?"

"Newhaven!"

"What are we going to do there?"

"I have no idea!"

Mike filled Reg in on what had happened and what they faced. Reg interrupted just once, when he asked if Smail had managed to get through to his wife.

"Smail is a man of his word, if he said he would, then I'm sure he has," Mike replied, as they got on the A264 and he was able to make good use of the open road. Mike had plugged his phone into the car, expecting to be able to use it as a sat nav, but the little blue dot never showed up to indicate where he was, so instead he used it as a static map, noting which turns they needed to make at which intersections, and concentrated instead on driving.

Reg had started out quite anxious in the passenger seat, holding the handle above the door, and liberally applying the front-seat passenger's side foot pedals. After about ten minutes of travel with no one else on the roads, he started to enjoy himself. "Nice car," he managed, after Mike had nailed the apex of one corner, steadily applying the gas for a smooth acceleration out of the bend. Mike had to admit he was enjoying himself. He had a mission, he had the ways and means of accomplishing it—or, at least, the most immediate part of it—and the driving was wholly keeping his mind occupied, so that he wasn't thinking about all the ways that things could go drastically wrong.

By and large, Mike stayed on his side of the road, but as the roads started to open out he made more and more use of the additional space to increase his speed. He was sensible around built up-areas, though their route by and large skirted around the various country towns and villages. In fact, it was at one such town where they saw the only other traffic on the road. As they approached a roundabout leading to a bypass, they could see the back of a police car heading straight ahead as they turned left. Mike kept off the accelerator a little after that and he could see Reg mulling things over out of the corner of his eye.

"So, Mike, what's the plan when we get to Newhaven? We get everybody lined up against the wall and then I pick our guy out? How is this all going to work?"

Mike now had to reveal what was missing from his plan—something he'd been dreading since they'd started their trip. He thought for a second, decelerating to negotiate the entrance to a roundabout before elegantly shifting through the gears as they headed alongside the river.

"The way I figure it, we'll pose as rich folk trying to escape the country and try to get on the boat. That will give us the chance to get on the boat and check out the other passengers. If our man is aboard we'll get word to the Home Office and try and get some support from the Navy, Coast Guard or someone in a helicopter. If not, we'll wrestle him to the ground and take him back to London ourselves."

Reg watched him carefully. "That sounds a little dangerous, Mike. I'll tell you what I'd like to do. We'll find the boat and try to get aboard. I'll identify our friend and give you the nod, and then get off the boat before it leaves harbour. I'll try and raise the alarm. Surely there's a policeman in Newhaven? Or if you have a phone number for the Home Office I can try and get in touch with them for you?"

Mike nodded as he approached yet another roundabout. "Yeah, it's a bit of an unknown—who knows how many of them on the boat will be the plotters? Sure, OK, your plan sounds better. I can always go on the boat and continue the chase there if needed. And you have to get back home, right?"

Reg nodded silently.

"Cool. OK, we can't be far from the town," Mike said as they approached a light industrial area, the road on both sides surrounded by warehouses and yards populated by assorted shipping containers. Mike could see a bridge coming up but didn't realise that the road leading up to it was off to their left until he was already past it and was underneath the bridge. "Oh no, I'll have to go back," he said.

"Nah, nah, you're OK," said Reg, indicating the intersection ahead. "This way just crosses the railway lines is all, hang a right here and it connects up."

"Ah, OK," said Mike, as they made their way over the railroad tracks, almost bottoming out the low-slung car in the process. The other side of the tracks led up to the bridge over the river that they'd be following for the last few miles, at various distances.

As they crossed the bridge, Mike looked to the left and saw the river mouth leading straight out to the channel through large concrete breakwaters on either side, and the marina tucked into the side to the right. Opposite the marina, on the left of the river was the ferry port, empty currently, the desolate, underutilised infrastructure in stark contrast to the yachts and cruisers on the right-hand side.

Mike turned left after the bridge, figuring that the marina would be somewhere between the river and the channel, so they'd be best served by following the river as closely as possible.

They made their way past a fish and chip shop before a yellow barrier blocked their path—or, at least, attempted to. Mike gave it a long glance and then with a cheeky grin drove under the barrier, continuing down the lane. The neighbourhood was very residential and they drove past modern homes with large windows, tightly packed in to maximise their sliver of river view. In contrast to a lot of the other towns that they had driven through, this one had the expected level of cars parked on the roads.

The road dog-legged left then right and before being surrounded by large apartment buildings, blocking the views of everyone else. Directly after them, the road ran alongside the sea again and now they could see the marina. The sun had lost its heat but was only now just beginning to set, still visible above the hills to their right. They could now see the boats in the marina, but Mike hadn't seen any buildings or entrances, so he asked Reg to keep an eye out as he drove along increasingly narrow roads.

They passed the entrance to Newhaven Fort on their right, and yachts on stilts in a yard on their left, before they finally came to the entrance to a car park tucked around a corner. They pulled in, the bottom of the car grinding a little against a pothole, and surveyed the car park. Aside from the signage warning that parking was for berth holders only, the car park could have passed for any upmarket car yard. There were Rolls-Royces, Bentleys, a smattering of Maserati's and a large contingent of Porsche Cayenne's.

"I think we're in the right place," said Mike.

They pulled into one of the few parking places left and got out. The facilities around there were a bit limited. Facing them beside the access to the marina wharves was a sullen building with a pair of large roller doors and a posterboard promoting Boats for Sale.

Now what? thought Mike. Do we start calling out 'cooee!'?

"Hullo, there!" bellowed someone from behind them. They spun around to see a crusty older man with white beard and tanned lined skin watching them from the pedestrian door of the building. "Can I help you?"

Mike gathered himself. "Would there be anyone willing to take us to France?"

The man looked them over and allowed that an agreement might be made. "As it happens there might be someone who would be willing to take you over tonight."

That was unexpected. "Uh, not noon tomorrow?" Mike asked.

The old man shook his head. "The tides," he said vaguely.

"How much?" asked Reg.

The old man pursed his lips. "Well, see, I don't think that there are that many alternatives, so I'm afraid the price will be a little steep."

"How steep?" asked Reg, raising one eyebrow.

"Well, see, you give me the car, and we'll call it even," responded the old man with a glint in his eye.

Reg's other eyebrow joined its partner and he turned to Mike. "Are you—"

"Done," said Mike. "When do we leave?"

"We're casting off at 7pm sharp, or whenever...our other passengers arrive," came the reply. That gave them half an hour.

"Is there food on board?"

The old man shook his head.

"The Implication has a galley, but no food. Plenty to eat in France though."

"OK, we'll go, but we'll hang onto the car to try and get something to eat. We'll be back though, so don't go anywhere, OK?"

The old man gave them a gleeful wink. "I'll be here! Don't you worry about that. But I wouldn't be late if I was you!"

They headed back to the car.

"Did you notice if the takeaways we passed on the way in were open?" asked Reg.

"We're not looking for food—we need a phone. If they're making a special trip there must be a reason, and the chances are that it's a mass escape. They're on the run. We've got to get in touch with Grayson."

"They might have a phone at the takeaways," said Reg slowly.

Mike shot him a glance and laughed at Reg's innocent look. "I guess we could have a look," he admitted, driving towards the fish and chip shop. Miraculously, it seemed to be open, and Mike parked in an otherwise empty car park overlooking the river and the bridge.

As they swung out of the car, Reg made a point of checking his pockets. "Uh... my wallet was taken, do you mind getting this one? I'll sort you out later."

"No problem, Reg," replied Mike as they entered the shop. "What can I get you?" They both peered up at the signage behind the counter. The prices seemed... a little steep. The man behind the counter had a cigarette hanging from his bottom lip and was watching them with a bored look on his face. He looked like he was two days through a three-day hangover.

"Yeah, those are the prices. No, I'm not having a laugh. If you don't like it, you're welcome to try somewhere else."

"I'll have whatever you're having, and a can of drink," said Reg very softly.

"Can I get two vegetarian spring rolls, a couple of pies and two cans of fizz?"

"Sure," came the reply as a pen and paper were used to calculate the bill. "That'll be seventy-five quid, please."

Mike already had a credit card out and leaned closer to the guy, lowering his voice. "If you let us use your phone, I'll make it an even hundred. I've got to call my wife."

The guy looked lazily from Reg to Mike and back, and then shrugged. "Whatever." He processed the payment, gestured to the phone behind the counter and disappeared into the kitchen. Mike made his way around the counter and picked up the phone, half expecting there to be no connection. He was relieved when the comforting dial tone met his ears. He asked Reg to keep an eye out for motorcycles on the bridge, hoping that if The Handler came to Newhaven he'd use the bridge and not approach from a different direction.

He got out Grayson's number and dialled.

He assumed the number was being redirected to Grayson's mobile because there was a series of clicks before a different background hiss gave way to plinking piano background music.

Reg hissed across the shop at him and Mike looked up in time to see a single headlight crossing the bridge. Reg's eyes grew wider as the headlight got brighter and then pulled up on the footpath outside the shop. The rider got off, took off his helmet and turned off the bike before coming inside.

The annoying tinkle of the on-hold music filled Mike's world as the man they were hunting walked calmly into the shop. Reg had been spot on with his description—average everything, with a sweep of dark hair. He could see him ask Reg a question and Reg answer before The Handler walked past him into the kitchen beyond. A few minutes later he came back out, nodded at Reg and put the helmet back on and headed towards the marina.

The tinkle of the bell on the door as it closed coincided with Grayson coming on the line. Reg was maintaining eye contact with Mike and very intently nodding as Mike started talking.

"Grayson! Listen, we don't have much time. The Handler is leaving the country and we're on the same boat as he is. We're leaving Newhaven for France at 7pm. Can you get someone to intercept the boat?"

"Well done, Mike, how sure are you that he's on board?"

"I've got an eye witness here that says it's him, so I'm pretty sure."

"I'll do what I can but whatever you do, do not get on the boat. If we have to, we'll send out an Apache from Wattisham or Farnborough to take it out before it reaches French waters. What kind of boat is it?"

"I don't know"

"Well, where in France is it going?"

"I don't know. The ferries here go to Dieppe, but I really don't know."

"Do you at least know its name?"

"The... Reg, what's the name of the boat? The Implication? The Implication."

"OK, and leaving Newhaven at 7pm? Right, OK, we'll take care of it. Thanks for this Mike. When this is all over we'll have a beer."

"You're paying. What do we do now?"

"Stay out of trouble—stay safe. Go home."

"Will do. Thanks, Grayson."

"Goodbye, Mike."

He hung up just as the shopkeeper brought their food, all wrapped in plain paper and loaded into a plastic bag. Reg got a can out of the fridge and asked what Mike wanted. Distractedly, Mike shrugged and so Reg got the same again and they nodded and thanked the shopkeeper as they left.

They walked to the car, and Mike filled Reg in on what Grayson had said.

Reg whistled when he got to the bit about the Apaches. "Wow, so they'll just blow it up? You definitely don't want to be on that boat!"

"I know, right? The fort is quite high up, maybe we could see from up there."

"Yeah but that gate is just beside the entrance to the marina, you don't want to have old whatshisface coming up and asking why we changed our minds, right?"

"Good point. So we wait until the boat leaves and then head up to the fort, keeping the lights off so we don't get seen. How does that sound?"

"Yeah, that might work. What's the time now?"

It was a few minutes after 7pm, so they ate their suppers in the car, winding the clock down.

"Were you really going to swap your car for a couple of seats to France? You could have swapped it for the best boat there."

Mike looked embarrassed. "Oh, it's not my car. I borrowed it." Realising how that looked, he shook his head and muttered, "Dad would be turning in his grave."

Reg nodded slowly. "So, after this, can you take me back home? I know someone who will be glad to see me, and it will be really nice to see her."

Mike was glad for the change of topic. "Yeah—ha! I take you out for a nice drive, we get dinner and now I'm taking you up to a make-out point to watch the fireworks, and you just want to go home."

Reg grinned. "I don't put out on the first date!"

The screeching of seagulls gave way to the sound of a powerful engine starting up in the marina and they both walked over to the river's edge and peered in its direction. They could just make out the boat which had started up, a sleek dagger of white, a little out of place amongst the comparatively drab yachts and smaller pleasure craft. They could see a group of four men walking along the jetty towards the boat. They had to go in single file because it was narrow, but talking amongst themselves, occasionally turning to make a point. Among them was The Handler, no longer in motorbike leathers but in T-shirt and jeans and holding what looked like a walkie talkie to his ear as he walked at the rear of the group. The guy on the boat called out and, while they couldn't hear the response, there was an abundance of shrugging followed by a bunch of laughter. They all got aboard and then the boat cast off, making its way slowly through the maze of jetties before reaching open water and accelerating.

Mike and Reg went back to the car and finished their meals. Wiping his hands on the wrapping paper, Mike collected the rubbish, deposited it in the bin, then jumped back in the car to head back along the road towards the marina building and the turn off for the fort. By this time, the direct sunlight was blocked by the hills. They took the turn off for the fort, Reg keeping an eye out for the old man as they passed the marina. The car park at the top of the hill was empty and the entrance to the fort was closed and locked, but the path led to the top of the fort, and so they parked the car and headed up the slope. The path continued around the fort and by the time they had clambered up the earth rampart which faced the sea and formed the outer wall of the fort, the sun was just setting. From their elevated viewpoint, they could see for miles in every direction. The arms of the breakwater extended a long way into the channel with a lighthouse at the furthest point. They sat on the old emplacement where guns had been installed to protect the country from invasion, but whether that had been against the Napoleonic French, Nazi Germans or Spanish Armada, Mike didn't know. The Implication was still visible, a flash of white at the head of the widening V as it headed out into the channel. Mike and Reg both scoured the skies for any sign of helicopters but didn't see any.

Reggie frowned. "They've stopped," he said.

Mike could see that he was right. The boat was dead in the water quite a way out. Just then, there was a broiling in the water near the gently drifting boat, and the conning tower of a submarine poked above the surface. The fat cigar of the rest of the submarine joined it on the surface. Reggie and Mike stared dumbfounded as the crew of the Implication made their way onto the submarine. The last man off the boat had tied something to the controls and as he stepped off he looked like he pulled a string. The Implication leapt forward and resumed its journey towards France, unmanned.

"We've got to tell Grayson. If he sends a helicopter, they won't be able to stop the submarine," said Mike. The submarine was already disappearing below the surface.

In the distance, they could hear the percussive thwap of helicopter blades. As they hurriedly made their way back towards the car they saw the dark shapes of the Apaches fly by against the light blue of the early evening sky. By the time they had got back into the car, they heard the echo of an explosion out in the Channel.

Mike wasted no time driving back to the takeaway shop, only to find the lights off inside and a sign on the door. The sign normally said Back in Five, but someone had crossed out the 'Five' in sharpie and replaced it with 'Never'. Mike tried the door but it was locked.

"Out of the way," said Reggie. He came barrelling past Mike, holding a metal rubbish bin as a battering ram and smashed the glass in the takeaway door. The last shards of glass dropped onto the floor in the still of the night. No alarm. In the distance, a dog barked once, but silence settled back on the sleepy town.

Reggie used the bin to clear the glass from the edges of the door and Mike carefully made his way inside. It was dark, the outside street lights only partially illuminating the interior, so Mike pulled out his phone and turned its torch on. He navigated his way to where he remembered the phone being and dialled Grayson again. Mike practically hopped from one foot to another waiting for Grayson to come onto the line and, when he eventually did, his eagerness to get the message out made it a single word of run together syllables. "TheHandlergotonasubmarine. He got away, Grayson!"

"I'm sorry, who is this? Is this you, Mike?"

"Yes! It's The Handler. On the boat. He got off. He got onto a submarine."

"Oh." A long pause. "Thank you, Mike." And then he hung up. Leaving Mike staring at the phone.

Reggie cleared his throat from the doorway. "Everything OK?"

"Come on, I'll take you home," Mike replied. The walk back to the car was like returning from a funeral, both men sombre and silent, alone with their thoughts. Mike flicked the headlights on and they made their way back to the country roads crisscrossing the south of England. Mike drove a lot more carefully now—there was no sense of urgency and the anti-climax of The Handler's escape soured any sense of achievement in finding him.

THE BARK

Mike eased off the accelerator on the way back to Eastwell Manor. Driving in the dark with no one else on the roads was substantially more nerve-wracking than the daylight drive to Newhaven. There was comfort in being able to see anyone else using the roads, and he had enjoyed being the only one on the roads, secure in the thought that he'd be able to see any other cars or pedestrians. On the way back, he suddenly realised that he could come to a bend and find who-knows-what on the road ahead. So he decided to keep his speed down to maintain some semblance of reaction time, just in case.

The car was a driver's delight, incredibly responsive and with great grip and although it would have been better to have been able to crank it up, Mike still enjoyed the journey back to Eastwell Manor. On the way he tried to prepare Reggie for the scene that they would encounter.

When they did pull into the driveway, Reggie didn't wait until the car had come to a full stop, swinging the door open and erupting into the quiet country night air calling Meredith's name. Mike parked, noticing that the petrol gauge was showing empty. Mike got out and followed the sound of Reggie's calls. He found him standing in front of the burnt out husk of the manor. He placed a consoling arm on his shoulders. "You can rebuild it," he said.

Reggie's confusion was clear in the waning moonlight. "Hmm? Oh! No, I was just trying to think where Meredith could be. Can you take me to the other golf course? Maybe she's still there."

"I don't know how much petrol we've got left, but sure."

They returned to the car and Mike handed Reggie his phone to navigate. But the car refused to start. Mike looked over at Reggie, his face illuminated by the light of the phone. He looked murderous. "It might be better that we're not driving around in the middle of the night, anyway," tried Mike. "Shall we recline the seats and try and get some sleep? We can get some gas in the morning and drive to the golf course then."

It took a few seconds, but Reggie regained his composure, the muscles clenching his jaw relaxing one by one. "That's probably a good idea," he allowed eventually.

A few minutes of exploring the seat controls later, they had made themselves as comfortable as they could in the cramped interior, and drifted off to sleep.

In the morning, Reggie lead the way along the driveway back to the lane they had driven up the previous night. As they reached the brick wall that had once held the black metal gate of Eastwell Manor, Reggie noticed the gleam of something plastic attached to it. He bounded over to it and the whooped.

He turned toward Mike, grinning. "They're OK," he said. "It's a message from Meredith saying that she's at the Duck's Bark."

Mike looked confused. "What's the Duck's Bark?" he managed.

"It's a gastropub. Our local. C'mon, it's not far."

Mike enjoyed the urgent walk along the country lanes to the pub. The sun illuminated the idyllic country scene of the morning mist over the rolling pastures, the occasional herd of cows beyond the hedgerows. Less than an hour later they were at the car park in front of the pub. There were still a couple of cars looking lonely in the car park, no lights were visible through the pub's windows. Reggie wasted no time, bounding up the steps to the door and trying to open it. When he found it was locked, he started banging vigorously.

It took a few minutes of banging before any sign of life inside became apparent. Reggie suddenly stopped knocking and backed away and Mike pretty quickly realised why. The long barrel of a gun was protruding from the open door, pointing directly at Reggie from the dark interior.

"Reginald? Is that you?" Robert asked, lowering the gun.

"Robert! We got the note at the Manor, is Meredith here?"

The lights behind Robert flicked on, and Mike could see past him into the interior of the pub. A number of children seemed to be milling around inside and they burst out the door past Robert to engulf Reggie. It turned out that they weren't all children after all—one middle-aged woman, two teens and a child all clung to one or other of Reggie's limbs as they all tried to talk at once.

Mike got a better look at them all as the mass of limbs and bodies rotated with one or other of them attracting Reggie's attention as he turned to talk with each of them in turn. The woman had buried her face into Reggie's chest and was gently crying. The older of the two girls was in her late teens or very early twenties and looked like she'd been in a fight with bruising all over her face. The boy was probably a little younger than her, a tall beanpole with what looked like the start of an afro. Finally, the little girl was very slim and clung like a limpet to one of Reggie's legs.

Robert had unloaded the shotgun and stood with it broken open and cradled in the crook of his arm, the barrels pointing at the ground. He had an enormous smile on his face and was joyfully watching the reunion. He noticed Mike looking at him and nodded a greeting. He came over to Mike and held out his right hand. "Robert," he introduced himself.

Mike took his hand and shook it. "Mike," he replied.

"Where did you find this guy?" Robert asked, indicating Reggie with a raised eyebrow.

"I tried to get to him before the uprising did, but I couldn't get there in time."

Sensing his self-reproach, Robert patted him on the shoulder. "It's OK, you got to him eventually. And he's OK now."

Mike thought of how close they'd come to apprehending The Handler. Objectively, he knew he should focus on the success of saving Uncle Reggie, but all he could feel was an empty void. "I guess," he said.

EPILOGUE

The beer with Grayson turned out to be a month later. In that time, the nation had begun to heal, with trials and breathless reporting of the death and destruction across the nation filling the newspapers and TV shows. It would take some time before things went back to normal though, as the mess of the destroyed stately homes and interrupted lines of inheritance needed untangling. Mike was meeting Grayson at his club in the middle of London, the resilient city bouncing back to business as usual more quickly than the rest of the country.

It was Mike's first time in a private club and he presented himself to the receptionist with no expectations. "I'm Mike Reid, here to meet Grayson."

The receptionist smiled and told him to follow her, leading him into the bowels of the Edwardian mansion, past portraits of bewhiskered pillars of community and commerce. In a lounge room of tall windows and low-slung leather chairs, Grayson greeted him with a firm handshake. "What would you like to drink? They have a lovely Macallan which will warm your cockles."

"Sure, if that's what you're drinking. And a beer chaser—it's still a little early for me to hit the spirits."

Grayson made arrangements, and they settled into the comfy armchairs. The lounge was about half full, a smorgasbord of white, middle-aged, balding men. "Nice place, though I thought I might have trouble getting in. It is rather... beige," he managed.

Grayson looked around and nodded ruefully. "Only so much appetite for change I'm afraid. Tradition and all that. Though I guess recent events have proven that the public might have more appetite for change than we gave them credit for, eh?"

Mike couldn't take it anymore. "So... what actually happened that night? With The Handler?"

Grayson looked apologetic. "Ah yes, that... We didn't have any handy submarine or anti-submarine assets nearby and by the time we vectored those resources that we did have to the route we believed their submarine would take, it was too late. They got away. Our current thinking is that they must have gone to Russia."

Mike thanked the receptionist who had delivered his drinks, taking a sip of the scotch. "So they got away. Surely that implicates the Russian government though?"

Grayson flashed a frown. "Ah, possibly," he responded eventually. "If we had evidence. We've expelled their diplomats and our relationship is one level above frosty, so there's not much more we can do at the moment. But we're certainly thankful for your assistance. You filled in a lot of the blanks in our knowledge."

"Did you track down how the AKs came into the country?"

Grayson looked downright shady, shifting uncomfortably in his seat. "Er, yes, embarrassingly. We'd intercepted a shipment of arms that the Russians had sent to Libya when our friend Gaddafi had been deposed and the militias were carving up the country. We still had a trade embargo in place, so when we intercepted the arms we confiscated them. Well, those were the containers that found their way into the country through Felixstowe and into the hands of the death squads. The investigation into how that happened and who was responsible has ground to a halt, unfortunately."

Mike smiled conspiratorially. "If you need an independent party to come in and ask the hard questions, I'm sure that my new firm would be only too happy for me to bring in an engagement of that size. And rest assured, I'd get to the bottom of it!"

Grayson smiled back. 'Oh, my dear boy, I'm sure you would. You'd be like a dog with a bone, I'm sure. No stone unturned! You seem to think it was some sort of inside job? But the people who would have been responsible would surely be those who would be on the receiving end of the guns, so what possible motivation would they have to arm those who would wish ill of them?"

"I would love to know though."

"I'm sure. Tell me how your companion fared—did he manage to make it back to his wife?"

"Reg? Yeah, there was a tearful reunion in the car park of the Duck's Bark." Grayson looked blankly back. "It's a gastropub with rooms near his manor. His wife was waiting there with their nephew and niece, and they had each thought the other was dead, so very emotional. That reminds me, I've got to chase up Smail. He was supposed to pass word to Meredith that Reg was OK."

"Oh?"

"Somehow word didn't get through. Between the kisses and hugs he was getting beaten around the ears something fierce. She packs a wallop for such a petite frame. Quite the woman. Fierce!"

"So all's well that ends well, hmmm?"

"Well... somewhat. Is anyone looking for The Handler? What was his real name? And what did he have to gain from provoking an uprising? Who else stood to gain from the uprising? Who supported it? If you knew about it, why didn't you stop it?" Mike paused, taking a long sip of beer without moving his eyes from Grayson's. "So, a few unanswered questions. A lot of which, only you can answer." He waited.

"Very good questions, Mike. Very astute," replied Grayson beckoning for another drink. "The Government of this country, and by that I don't mean our esteemed representatives in Westminster, but the people who get things done, have got an issue with representation. Like this room, they're... how did you put it? Beige. Yes, beige. Very fitting. So the Home Office is doing very well with increasing representation, but other areas are not doing quite as well and in senior positions everyone is doing quite poorly. That's the problem when you don't have a strong pipeline. You ignore people and hold them down and exclude them and then when you get a senior role open, there's no one but Etonians who are eligible. And look where that leads us." His drink came and he paused to savour the aroma, taking his time with the first sip before putting it down with a satisfied sigh. "And sometimes you can't grow from within because nobody on the team is quite ready yet, or they don't have quite the right combination of skills."

Mike nodded thoughtfully, not really following, but waiting to see where this was going.

"And when that happens, you sometimes have to go outside the shop. To find someone who has investigative skills and knows their way around a database. And who has 'Deeply Vetted' security clearance. And can lead teams. And cares about justice."

"And is black?"

Grayson seemed bemused. "That did come up when we discussed you. We can't compare you to someone who has all your skills, traits, experience and attitudes and who is white, because they don't exist. And what really pushed us over the edge wasn't the fact that you give us a tick in the right box for 'BAME Senior Manager', but your drive for justice in apprehending The Handler."

Mike knew the acronym well. BAME stood for Black, Asian or Minor Ethnicity. A more positive way of saying 'Non-white'. A phrase defining in terms of what you are, rather than what you are not.

"So you're asking me to give up a very nice job in an industry that I've been carving out my reputation in for the last ten years, and you want me to join an organisation where I would be one of the only... BAME people in a senior role, where the organisation is run by people who see me as a direct threat."

Grayson's bemusement increased. "Yes."

"And here's the kicker," Mike said, getting more intense. "You want me to get paid a civil service salary for the privilege?"

Grayson let out a laugh. "Yes!"

Mike petulantly leant back in his chair. Then took a long swallow of his beer. "Let me sleep on it. But if I take the job, I'm going after The Handler every chance I get."

Grayson leant back in his chair, raising his glass. "I would expect nothing less," he said as he took a swallow.

ABOUT THE AUTHOR

C.G. Lambert was born the second of seven children and raised in South Auckland, New Zealand. His pre-writing career consisted of applying for whatever job sounded interesting, leading to time as an International Banker, a Music Manager, Web Developer and Analytics Manager. He loves travel (you can read about it at etrip.tips), holds dual citizenship (NZ/UK), a Bachelor of Arts and an MBA. He currently resides in the UNESCO City of Literature—Edinburgh—with his long term partner.

You can find out more at cglambert.com

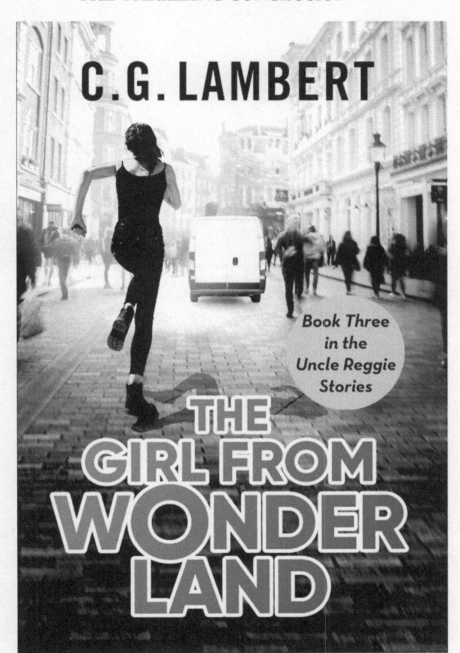

THE THRILLING CONCLUSION

C.G. LAMBERT

Book Three
in the
Uncle Reggie
Stories

THE
GIRL FROM
WONDER
LAND

HOW IT ALL BEGAN

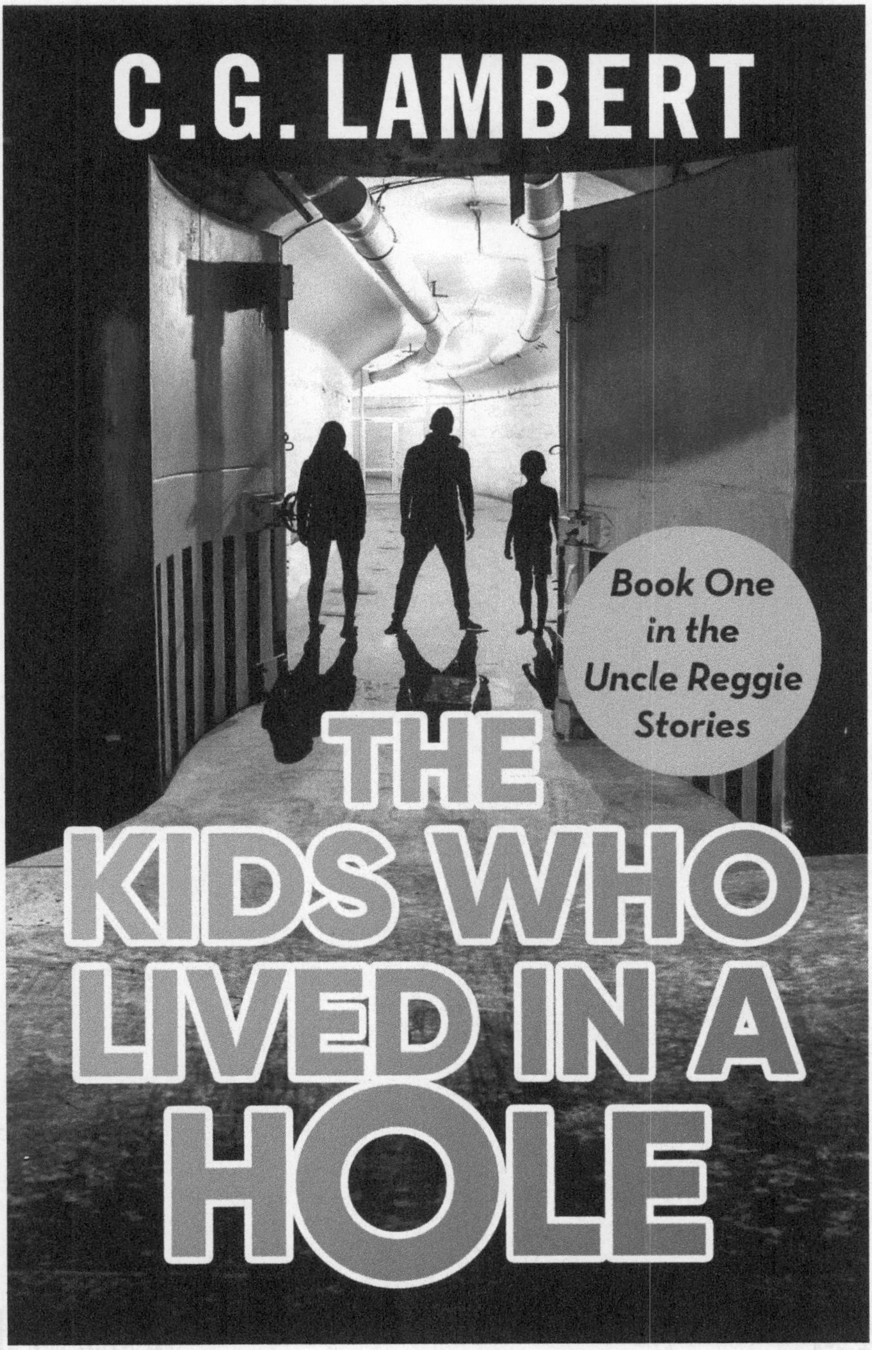

CPSIA information can be obtained
at www.ICGtesting.com
Printed in the USA
LVHW032046280721
693947LV00015B/883/J

9 781914 531118